Witches (un)welcome!

First published in Great Britain in 2019 by Simon & Schuster UK Ltd
A CBS COMPANY

1 3 5 7 9 10 8 6 4 2

Simon & Schuster UK Ltd
1st Floor, 222 Gray's Inn Road
London
WC1X 8HB

www.simonandschuster.co.uk
www.simonandschuster.com.au
www.simonandschuster.co.in

Simon & Schuster Australia, Sydney
Simon & Schuster India, New Delhi

A CIP catalogue record for this book is available from the British Library.

PB ISBN: 978-1-4711-7560-2
eBook ISBN: 978-1-4711-7561-9

This book is a work of fiction.   Names, characters, places and incidents are either
the product of the author's imagination or are used fictitiously.   Any resemblance
to actual people living or dead, events or locales is entirely coincidental.

Printed and bound by CPI Group (UK) Ltd, Croydon, CR0 4YY

MIX
Paper from
responsible sources
FSC® C020471

KAYE UMANSKY

Witches (Un)welcome!

Illustrated by
ASHLEY KING

To Ivy-Rose, Orlaith and Nainsi

PICKLES' RULES
OF CUSTOMER SERVICE

1. BE FRIENDLY

2. PRETEND THAT THE CUSTOMER IS ALWAYS RIGHT

3. BE A GOOD LISTENER

4. KEEP PEOPLE CHATTING

5. BE SYMPATHETIC

6. USE A SOOTHING TONE WITH THE TRICKY ONES

7. ALWAYS BE HELPFUL

8. STAY OPEN WHENEVER POSSIBLE

9. ALWAYS HAVE A HANDY HANKY

10. USE FLATTERY

11. DRAW ATTENTION TO A BARGAIN

12. NEVER SHOW SURPRISE

13. NEVER SHORT CHANGE

14. BE EFFICIENT

15. USE THE HARD SELL ONLY AS A LAST RESORT

16. ALWAYS HAVE CHANGE

17. DISPLAY THINGS NICELY

18. DO NOT GET INTO ARGUMENTS WITH CUSTOMERS

19. NEVER SHOUT

20. KEEP YOUR SENSE OF HUMOUR

MAGENTA SHARP'S THREE RULES OF WITCHCRAFT

1. Read Instructions
2. Follow Recipe
3. Make It Work

SOME THINGS YOU NEED TO KNOW
BEFORE WE GET STARTED...

There are three important things you need to know about Elsie Pickles:

1. Elsie lives in Smallbridge – a boring country town with a small bridge. Smallbridge is not a magical sort of place. When magic occurs, people don't approve. They like an uneventful life. No surprises. No upsets. There are unspoken rules about noise, meal times, clothes, respectable occupations and the proper times to get up and go to bed. Hair is only let down on approved

bank holidays. Even then, the fireworks are over by ten. No need to go mad.

2. Elsie helps her dad, Albert, in the family shop, called Pickles' Emporium. Despite the grand name, the Emporium is a small shop down a side alley, full of cheap, boring things. People go there to chat and not spend much. You don't get rushed, like in other shops. That's because Albert is very hot on customer service. Elsie knows all his rules by heart. She doesn't mind her job. There are worse things than working with your dad. But not long ago she started wishing things could liven up a bit, like in books. Just something *different*. And then Magenta Sharp blew into town and definitely made things *different*. Because now...

3. Elsie is learning to be a witch. She didn't expect that last one. It just kind of happened after Magenta's visit.

Known locally (and rather sniffily) as 'that Red Witch Woman', people disapprove of Magenta Sharp for the following reasons:

1. She's a witch.
2. She wears red. If you must be a witch, at least look like one.
3. She wasn't born and bred in Smallbridge. Acts snooty.
4. She brings bad weather with her. On purpose.
5. She lives in Crookfinger Forest, which is lawless, sprawling and untidy.
6. She resides in a mysterious

tower that is rumoured to *move about!* Moving towers are against Smallbridge planning laws.

But Elsie finds Magenta fascinating. After their first meeting, Elsie agreed to look after the tower while the witch was away. Nuisance, the town's stray dog went with her to make sure she was OK (and also because he thought Elsie might have sausages to give him – sausages are his favourite) and now his heart belongs to Elsie. He does his own doggy thing during the day, but at night he sleeps in the doorway of the Emporium. (He won't come in, though. He's an outside dog.)

Other important things that you need to know
are:

MAGIC

Elsie didn't mean to mess about with magic.
But now she's started, she doesn't want to stop.
Of course, magic is unpredictable and things
don't always turn out as planned – but Elsie has
a knack for it.

THE TOWER

The tower is wonderful. Sometimes, it seems
almost alive. There is a magical larder that
produces endless cakes; a wardrobe containing
new clothes; a spelloscope on the roof, so you
can spy on your neighbours (who include the
Howler sisters – two sweet little old ladies with
tails and a thing about buckets!) and a room of

stars containing a sparkling wheel, which you turn to make the tower move. (Actually, you don't have to bother with that. It's all an illusion – but the tower likes to put on a show.)

CORBETT

Corbett is the traditional raven that comes with a tower. He's surly and grouchy and looks down his beak at other birds, especially pigeons. But Elsie can always get round him.

JOEY AND SYLPHINE

When she was tower-sitting Elsie became great friends with Joey the post boy, and Sylphine Greenmantle (real name: Aggie Wiggins) who dresses like a wood sprite and dances barefoot in the moonlight, although she probably shouldn't. At the end of her week at the tower, Elsie went home with a bulging purse, a pair of magic dancing shoes and a whole new set of magical skills that she had to keep a secret because the people of Smallbridge just wouldn't approve at all.

Her life went back to normal ... boring days ... weeks ... months...

Then, on May Day, one of the few fun days of the year, the Red Witch showed up again! This time, she wanted Elsie's help sorting out her mail order business, *Sharp Spells On Tap*, which was *not* going well. Lots of angry customers, a chaotic list of orders and a very grumpy Magenta. Well, Elsie jumped at the chance to help and learn more magic. So she spent another exciting week at the tower where she saved the business, learned new spells, visited a magical superstore, put a very rude genie in his place and dealt with some tricky crowd/animal control.

Elsie also learnt the secret of *taking a shortcut*. That's witch talk for vanishing on the spot and popping up somewhere else. A very useful trick...

And, now that we're all caught up with the important things, let's find out what's in store for Elsie this time...

Chapter One
DON'T DO IT TOO OFTEN

'The trouble is,' Elsie said to Joey, 'I do it too often.'

It was opening time on a sunny Saturday and they were both leaning on the counter, deep in conversation. Nuisance was sitting upright in the doorway, eyes fixed lovingly on his two favourite people. Elsie's dad was upstairs ironing his apron.

Joey had come to deliver the shop's post – two coupons, some bills and an advertisement for rivets – although it was just an excuse to come

and see Elsie really. Smallbridge wasn't officially on his round. Usually he stuck to Crookfinger Forest. Elsie had given a happy squeal when she'd opened the shutters and seen him waiting outside with Nuisance.

Elsie was always happy to see Joey. He was one of the few people she could talk to about magic. He wasn't disapproving in a Smallbridge way. He lived in the forest, where they did things differently.

'How do you do it?' he asked. 'Is it easy?'

'Very. You simply close your eyes, picture where you want to go, think the secret word and there you are.'

'Brilliant!' said Joey. 'Talk about useful. I'd do it all the time if I could. What's the secret word?'

'I can't tell you. A witch has to whisper it in

your ear.'

'Well, you're a witch, whisper it to me.'

'I'm still learning. And it's not just about the *word*. You have to be able to picture where you're going, to think carefully about where you want to be.'

'Oh, well, I'd be no good at that,' said Joey. 'I never notice what's around me. I used to do my round with my eyes closed, when I got bored. That was before I got Bill to keep me company.'

He looked down fondly at the wire shopping basket at his feet. It was just sitting there being a basket – but there was something about its basketiness that wasn't quite normal. It looked … *alert*. Eager. Like it was waiting for someone to throw it a ball.

Joey had fallen in love with this particular basket on a never-to-be-forgotten trip to the magical superstore called the Sorcerer's Bazaar, where all the baskets floated. He had taken it home claiming that it would be a big help on the post round. But really he had thought it would be fun to have around. It was always up for a game. It could do tricks. It had personality. Nobody knew why he called it Bill.

'Anyway,' said Elsie. 'I'm stopping. No more shortcuts. Magenta says it's lazy.'

'What's so bad about that? Personally, I've done enough walking to last me a lifetime.'

'I think she meant you shouldn't overuse magic just because it's easy,' said Elsie. 'Some things should be done the slow, normal way. Like making soup or walking up stairs or tidying your bedroom.'

Taking a shortcut wasn't the only thing Elsie could do. She had three solid little spells at her fingertips. Showers of eggs, rains of frogs and storms in teacups. They were the first spells she'd learned and now she could do them perfectly, with fancy variations. And there were a few new spells she was experimenting with. Of course, she was careful not to do any of this where people might see. Smallbridge wouldn't be comfortable with it.

But ...

Only the other day she had set off a tiny storm in a mug of tea, just for fun, and Mr Sourman had seen. He wasn't one of Elsie's favourite customers. His personality suited his name. He had been taking so long to choose his exciting purchase (a box of matches) that Elsie had forgotten he was still there. She'd given a hasty cough to disguise the tiny rumblings of thunder and got rid of the storm with a snap of her fingers. But Sourman saw all right.

Another time, alone and bored in the shop, Elsie had conjured up three small frogs and sat them in a line along the counter. One wore glasses, one carried a tiny handbag and one wore a straw hat and

played a guitar. She was getting really good at frogs. She had looked up to see Mrs Snoring standing in the doorway, her mouth an 'O' of horror. Elsie managed to convince her it was a trick of the light, but it was a near thing.

Then there was the time she had made a chocolate egg appear out of thin air to stop her brother, baby Todd, crying, and got some very odd looks from a group of people queuing for the butcher's.

Magic had become so automatic that sometimes Elsie forgot it was supposed to be a secret and just did it.

'*Don't do it too often,*' Joey mused. 'People always say that about fun stuff. Don't eat sweets too often. Don't stay up all night too often. Don't eat ice cream for breakfast or send off for a camel too often.'

'Exactly— send off for a *camel*?'

'Actually, I don't want one now. Not now I've got Bill. But, look, don't feel guilty. Enjoy yourself.'

'Hm. Anyway, tell me what's going on in the forest. How are Magenta, Corbett and Sylphine?'

'I've only been to the tower once since you left,' said Joey. 'There hasn't been any post and Her Witchiness doesn't appreciate friendly visits.'

'There's been no post?' Elsie frowned. 'None?'

'Nope. A couple of days after you went home, I got summoned. She gave me a bunch of letters that needed sending, yelled something about *having had enough* and slammed the door in my face.'

'Don't tell me,' said Elsie with a sigh. 'They were rude notes telling the customers that

Sharp Spells On Tap was no more, so get lost and never contact her again?'

Sharp Spells On Tap was a good name for a magical mail-order business. It implied an efficient concern that would guarantee a fast, steady stream of well-priced spells, with no cause for complaint. In reality, it was a disorganised mess, run from a chaotic office in a magical moving tower, and Magenta was a hopeless businesswoman. Her spells were excellent, but they hardly ever arrived because the parcel had the wrong stamps, blew up or simply disappeared. As orders backed up and the complaints began arriving, she just got angrier.

'I'm sorry, Elsie,' Joey said. 'After all you did. All that tidying. All those letters you wrote and potions you brewed up.'

'I left it all organised,' said Elsie.

'I know.'

'The bills were paid, the backlog of orders was cleared and the Magic Board didn't take away her licence.'

'I know.'

'I made sure she had everything she needed to make up the next batch of spells. And she had Corbett to help her. All they had to do was keep up with the orders and not throw customers' letters on the fire.'

'You know Her Witchiness,' said Joey. 'She gets bored. Suddenly loses interest. But now it seems she's bored with doing nothing. Impossible to live with, Corbett says.'

'You've seen Corbett, then?' asked Elsie.

Joey nodded. 'Yesterday. He saw me doing my

round and flew down to share my sandwiches.'

'How about Sylphine? Have you seen her?'

'Not for a while. She's visiting her grandma.'

'That's nice.'

'Not really. Her granny's really strict. She tells her to stop with the airs and graces and change her silly made-up name of Sylphine back to plain old Aggie. She makes her wear sensible clothes and take the flowers out of her hair. She forbids barefoot, moonlit dancing and any talk of unicorns. And she's not allowed cake.'

'Poor Sylphine. All the things she likes best,' said Elsie. 'Talking, dancing, unicorns and cake.'

'Anyway, I'd better go, I have to get home and fix Bill. One of his wires is loose, it's making him float lopsided.' Joey gave the basket a little nudge with his foot. 'Show Elsie your loose wire.'

Obediently, Bill bobbed up and hung in the air, wobbling slightly.

Footsteps came clumping down the flight of steep stairs from the attic. Elsie's dad, Albert, was coming to work in his newly-ironed apron that said: **Pickles' Emporium. Where Customer Service Always Comes First.**

Bill dropped to the floor and froze. This was Smallbridge. Not a place for baskets to be showing off their floating skills.

'Well, now, look who's here!' exclaimed Albert. 'Brought us some mail, have you, young man? Won the lottery, have we? Are we millionaires?' He gave a little chuckle.

'Hello, Mr Pickles,' said Joey. 'No, 'fraid not, ha ha.'

'No message from a Certain Someone needing our Elsie to help out again?'

Albert missed his only daughter when she went off into the forest, on what he thought of as those *mumbo-jumbo jaunts* of hers and came back home with funny new ideas. But on the other hand, she clearly enjoyed herself and Albert couldn't deny that she was well paid for her efforts.

'No,' said Joey. 'No message, Mr Pickles. I just dropped by to say hello.'

'Well, good to see you, lad. Need anything while you're here? Nails? Soap? Pencil with a rubber on the end? Or maybe one of these lovely vases for your mum?' He pointed to a stack of hideous green glass vases.

'No, thanks, Mr Pickles.' said Joey. 'She's already got one. Best be off. Bye, Elsie.'

And with that, he picked Bill up by the handle, just as you would a normal basket. The bell above the door tinkled – and he was gone.

Elsie gave a sigh. Seeing Joey reminded her of all the things she missed. If she could make a list, it would go like this:

I MISS:

My friends
Living in a magic tower in a forest
Corbett
Genies and elves and old ladies with wolf tails
My own room
My own bed
Cake for breakfast

Helping sort Magenta out

Messing about with magic

Right now, all those things seemed very far away.

Chapter Two
SHOPKEEPING

Later that morning, Elsie was alone in the shop, holding the fort while Albert nipped out to deliver a parcel. Saturday mornings usually started slowly. The Emporium always opened at nine on the dot, but nobody drifted in much before ten.

First to arrive was Mrs Snoring. She was returning a green glass vase which appeared to have a small crack in it. Elsie replaced it instantly. Albert had mistakenly ordered two hundred of the hideous things instead of twenty. They were stacked high on the floor by the door so that you couldn't miss them. There were many more in the basement.

Next to arrive was Mrs Lardy, who knew Mrs Snoring. Mrs Lardy had come to purchase a packet of paper serviettes in honour of an old friend called Sonia, who was coming to dinner with her husband, Ted. Mrs Snoring thought she might have met Sonia once, but wasn't sure. She certainly didn't recall Ted. Mrs Lardy embarked on a long description of Ted, in which the word *grey* appeared more than once. While they were chatting, the shop bell announced the arrival of Mr Sourman, back for another box of matches.

'What do you do – ? burn them?' joked Elsie. He didn't smile. Just gave her

a sour look. The incident with the storm had clearly not been forgotten.

'I was going to do fish pie,' said Mrs Lardy, 'but Sonia's allergic to fish. She only let me know this morning.'

'I call that rude,' chipped in a new voice. It belonged to Miss Winnie Whippet, who always wore a woolly scarf, even in summer, and suffered from a lot of ailments. 'People are so thoughtless. My lodger's always banging the door and bringing on one of my headaches.'

'You could do chops,' suggested Mrs Snoring to Mrs Lardy. 'Nice and easy.'

'They come in the night. The headaches,' Miss Winnie Whippet said to Elsie. 'First the indigestion wakes me, then my knee starts to play up and suddenly I've got a headache.'

30

'Goodness,' said Elsie, Customer Service Rule Five clicking in. 'Poor you. Can I get you something? Stomach powder? Bandage?'

'Chops *would* have been a possibility,' continued Mrs Lardy. 'Except I think Ted's a vegetarian.'

'Oh, now, that *is* awkward,' sympathized Mrs Snoring. 'I suppose it'll have to be cauliflower cheese.'

'Cheese brings me out in a rash,' said Miss Winnie Whippet. 'Mainly the blue ones. Stilton. Gorgonzola...'

Elsie stood behind the till, joining in where necessary, nodding and shaking her head in the right places, bright-eyed and helpful, the very picture of perfect customer service. But beneath the counter, her fingers were just itching to bring down a shower of comedy frogs. Not to be mean. Just to jolly things up a bit.

Slowly the morning dragged on. Old Mrs Trout tottered in, together with her mother-in-law, Very Old Mrs Trout. Together, their ages added up to one hundred and seventy. To Elsie, it felt like that was the amount of minutes they took to count out eighteen pennies for a bargain tea towel with a chicken design.

At one point, an angry-looking man with a flat cap and a black beard marched in, snatched up a hammer, slammed down coins, and marched out again.

At long last, the clock on the town hall struck midday.

'So,' said a familiar voice. 'That's how you spend your mornings, is it?'

And there, suddenly, was Magenta Sharp, standing by the stack of hideous vases. Her red hair and scarlet cloak clashed horribly with the green. In one red-gloved hand dangled a black, shiny top hat – the sort that rabbits jump out of.

'Magenta!' exclaimed Elsie. 'I didn't notice you arrive.'

'I've been here for ages. I was wearing my Hide-Me Hat. Want to try?'

She handed over the hat. Elsie took it in her hands and looked inside. No rabbit. She put it on, feeling a bit like a circus ring master.

'Now look down.'

Elsie did as she was told – and her head swam! She was gone! She could feel the hat on her head and her feet on the floor, so she was definitely *there* – but at the same time, she wasn't. It made her feel a bit queasy, so she reached up and took the hat off. To her relief, she was back again.

'It makes you dizzy at first,' said Magenta,

taking it back. 'But you get used to it. I bought this one ages ago at the Sorcerer's Bazaar. They only had it in black. I heard they do them in red now, but it's a long way to go for a hat. I'd have to take the tower and go through the whole moving ritual. Such a performance.'

'Can't you take a shortcut?'

'I'm cutting down on shortcuts. I told you, they make a witch lazy.'

'How did you get here, then?'

'Well, all right. But it's my last one today.'

'I saw Joey this morning,' said Elsie. 'He tells me you've closed down Sharp Spells. Have you?'

'Yes,' said Magenta. 'All that having to get the right *stamps* and the *right* sized jars and wrapping up the wretched *parcels* and slaving over a cauldron all night making up spells with only that miserable bird to help. It was time to move on.'

'I thought you wanted the world to experience your amazing products.'

'I do. Just not at the expense of my sanity. Look, I know you did your best. Elsie. I won't say I'm sorry because I make it a rule never to apologize. But I'm grateful for your efforts.'

'You're welcome,' said Elsie. 'I enjoyed it. But as my dad says, retail isn't for everyone.'

'Well, it certainly comes easily to *you*,' said Magenta. 'You make it look like the easiest job in the world. Prop up the counter, listen to nonsense, put things in paper bags and take people's money.'

'There's a bit more to it than that.'

'Like what?'

'Well – you have to order the stock and do the accounts and keep the shelves full and watch out for shop lifters and be nice even when you don't feel like it—'

'Yes, well, you can get an assistant to do all that.' Magenta waved a red-gloved hand. 'Shop-keeping beats mail order any day. That's plain to see. Easy money for doing nothing. Shame about the customers, of course. Unbelievably dreary, aren't they? But then, so is your stock.' Magenta ran her eyes around. 'Nails. Buckets. Clothes pegs. Those hideous green vases. I mean.'

'True,' said Elsie. 'But that's the kind of thing people in Smallbridge want.'

'Do they?' said Magenta. 'Do they really? What do you think would happen

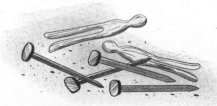

if you offered them something completely different?'

The shop bell tinkled, the door opened and in walked Albert.

'Sorry I'm late, pet, how's— oh!' He stopped short. 'Witch Sharp! It's good to meet you in person at last. Elsie's told us a lot about you. All good, of course, ha, ha.'

Magenta looked blank. She wasn't good at small talk.

'Now, then.' Albert switched briskly to salesman mode. 'Are you looking for anything in particular? We have an excellent selection of tea towels, allow me to show you.' He bustled off down the aisle. 'Elsie, show Witch Sharp the vases. They're selling like hotcakes. We can't guarantee to get any more.'

'Dad...' said Elsie.

'One moment, pet, I'm just finding a chicken tea towel for Witch Sharp.'

'But, Dad…'

'What?'

'She's gone, Dad.'

And she had.

Chapter Three
A NEW SHOP!

Sunday in Smallbridge was the dullest day of the week. All the shops were closed and so was the library. That left nowhere to go. There was a small statue of a sheep to climb on in the town square, but that was strictly for the little kids.

Traditionally, everyone had a lie-in. But not for *too* long, because there were potatoes to peel for lunch. To fill up the rest of the day, the selection of thrilling activities consisted of a snooze on the sofa or a stroll on Smallbridge Common – a flat, grey nothingness with no trees, no duck pond, no flowers, not even a bench to sit on. And that was Sunday, apart from putting out the bins.

Like the rest of Smallbridge, the Pickles tried to have a lie-in, but never really could because the boys were up – Arthy, Toby and baby Todd, Elsie's three small brothers. After breakfast, Elsie or her mum, Tilda would take them to the square to climb on the sheep. (Albert stayed in bed, and who can blame him?)

This particular Sunday, it was Tilda's turn to take the boys. Elsie stayed behind to clear away the breakfast dishes, give Nuisance his morning sausage and put the rubbish bins out.

It was a pleasant enough day when she pushed open the door and stepped out with the first bin. Blue sky, mild breeze. A perfectly normal, quiet Sunday morning – except for Nuisance. He came bounding up and leaped at her, barking loudly. He was always delighted to see Elsie, but this morning his greeting was particularly frenzied.

'Yes, yes, nice to see you too. Stop the racket, will you? I'll get your

sausage in a minute, just let me dump this bin.'

Pickles' Emporium was tucked away down a dark, narrow alley off the main street. For a shop, this wasn't ideal. There was no passing trade, because the alley went nowhere. But at least the rent was cheap. And the shop had been there a long time so people knew where to come if they suddenly found themselves in need of a tea strainer or a hideous vase.

The Emporium's bins were always placed at the very end of the alley, where weeds and nettles grew high on a patch of waste land. It was fast turning into the unofficial town tip, with a dumped armchair and two old tailor's dummies, but nobody cared because the alley bent round in a curve so it couldn't be seen from the high street. Carl the council worker sometimes left his wheelbarrow there. Once or twice, someone left a goat tied up overnight. Just a forgotten patch of waste land…

Which was gone!

In its place was a shop. You knew it was a shop because it had a large sign saying so.

There, emblazoned above the doorway, in big, red, twinkly letters were the words:

The shop door, window shutters and roof were all red. The wall consisted of red stripes on a white background, like a circus tent. There was so much red, it made your eyes hurt. It was garish. It was dazzling. In a weird sort of way, it was quite wonderful.

There were posters plastered all over the walls. They said:

'Oh!' gasped Elsie, dropping the bin with a clatter. '*Now* look what she's gone and done!'

Nuisance twitched his nose and licked Elsie's hand.

'Stay there,' Elsie said. 'I won't be long. I know you're hungry.'

She walked right up and knocked firmly on the closed door.

'Go away. I'm not open!'

'It's me,' said Elsie, pushing open the door.

Instead of the usual jingling shop bell, from somewhere overhead came a mournful hooting, like a lonely sea monster with tummy ache.

'What d'you think?' demanded Magenta. 'Too depressing? Leave the door open, I'm experimenting.'

She was sitting on a chair with her red boots propped up on a highly-polished wooden counter. On the counter was a large, ornate till. The rest of the space was taken up with piles of unopened cardboard boxes. The walls were bare. No shelves. Just counter, chair, fancy till and boxes. Plus the two old tailor's dummies from the tip.

'What's wrong with a bell?' asked Elsie.

'Too boring. I considered a witchy cackle, but it's a bit corny, don't you think? I'm after something mystic. Something that speaks of

the wonders to be found within.'

Elsie stared around. 'Something that sounds like cardboard boxes, then. That's all I see within.'

'Yes, well, I haven't unpacked yet, have I? What about this one?'

She muttered something under her breath, and waggled a finger in the air. There came a low, deep, sonorous chime that made both of them jump. It was like a doorbell in a vampire's castle and the echo went on for ages.

D-O-O-O-O-O-O-O-O-O-O-N-N-NG!

'No,' said Elsie. 'Unless you want the customers to die of fright every time they come in.'

'Mmm. It is a bit full on. Some sort of elvish horn, perhaps? The hoot of an owl? Scary, high-pitched tittering?'

'No. Just have a normal shop bell. That's what

people are used to.'

'Mm. Maybe you're right. So what do you think? About all *this*!' Magenta swept her arm around. 'My shop.'

'Well, I *like* it,' said Elsie carefully. 'But – um – why?'

'Why not? It's exactly what this boring little town needs. A local magic shop selling an excellent, hand-picked range of spells at reasonable prices.'

'I'm . . . just not sure Smallbridge is the right place. People are a bit unsure around wit— I mean newcomers. They're not used to red pop-up shops. How did you do it?'

'Ah.' Magenta swung her legs down from the counter, leaned forward and waggled a long red finger. 'Good question. You're asking how I created a unique magic shop and fitted it into a weirdly-shaped space down a narrow alley in the dark. All in a single night.'

'Yes,' said Elsie. 'All that.'

'Well,' said Magenta. 'Complicated big stuff like this normally means days of dreary research in the Magical Archives, where they won't let you take sandwiches. Endless hours copying down recipes. You have to learn difficult chants and order up loads of obscure spell ingredients, most of which are impossible to get. Plus, you can't fit shops into awkwardly-shaped spaces just like that. It takes skill. You have to start small. Fit chicken coops into funny-shaped gateways. Work up to putting potting sheds into problematic corner allotment plots. Things like that.'

'Gosh,' said Elsie. 'That sounds awfully hard.'

'It is. So I'm lucky I got sent this!'

Magenta gave a triumphant smile, reached under the counter and placed something on the counter. It was the size and shape of a small brick, but unlike a brick, it was smooth, grey and shiny, with three little holes one side. A single green light blinked on and off in the first of the holes. It was gently humming. Well, purring.

'What is it?' asked Elsie.

'The Spellatron 3000. Arrived yesterday. A new sort of magic. It does everything for you.

My sister sent it, of all people. Saw it advertised in a catalogue and thought of me.'

'It doesn't look that magical. There are no sparkles or fizziness or strange smells.' Elsie frowned down at the strange object. She couldn't put her finger on it, but there was something about it she didn't like. 'Where are the instructions?'

'There aren't any.'

'Where's the on-off button?'

'There isn't one.'

'I thought that was the first rule of witchcraft,' said Elsie. 'Read the instructions, follow the recipe and make it work. And know how to stop if things are going wrong. That's what you said.'

'Well, yes. But like I said, this is a new sort of magic. No instructions needed. Instant results. I simply told it what I wanted the shop to look like and where I wanted it to go and, hey presto, here it is, all red and sparkly.'

'So you took a shortcut?' said Elsie.

'Look,' said Magenta, looking slightly uncomfortable, 'I wanted a shop, I was in a hurry, now I've got one. And it's just how I imagined. I've only just seen it myself, five minutes ago. That's why I haven't started unpacking boxes.'

'Why didn't you get the Spellatron 3000 to put up some shelves?' asked Elsie.

'Because you need to say where they go. And we need to handle the stock ourselves.'

'*We*? I can't work here and at the Emporium,' Even as she said the words, Elsie felt a pang of disappointment. It would be such fun to work in a real life magic shop … but she couldn't leave her dad, could she?

'Fine,' Magenta sighed. 'Then I shall advertise

for an assistant first thing tomorrow. But you have to help me set things up today.'

'Well, I suppose I could stay for a little while…' Elsie said. But inside, she thought, *Yes! I'll help. I can't wait to see what's in the boxes! I want to organise the shelves! When can we start!*

Magenta clapped her hands. 'This is wonderful, isn't it? I have to say I'm quite excited.'

There came a flapping noise and Elsie looked round to see Corbett flying through the doorway.

'Coming in to land!'

His black feathers brushed her ear and he was on her shoulder. His claws gripped gently. It was good to have him back there.

'Hello, Corbett,' Elsie said. 'Nice to see you.'

'I've come to see the latest fad.' He stared around and gave a sniff. 'Hmm.'

'Go on,' said Magenta. 'Open your doomy beak and admit it's impressive.'

'Fancy on the outside,' admitted Corbett 'Gaudy. Catches the eye. You can't miss it. But there's a lot left to do in here, isn't there? By the way, there's a couple of little kids outside gawping in.'

'Well, they can shoo. I'm not open until tomorrow.'

Magenta stood up and swept out through the door. There came

two small screams and scampering sounds.

'I told her.' Corbett sighed and shook his glossy black head. 'I said a magic shop in Smallbridge was a bad idea. She said everyone needs magic in their lives and it'll be good to shake the place up. What do *you* think?'

'People won't like it,' said Elsie. 'Magic's not a Smallbridge kind of thing.'

'She wouldn't even have thought about opening a shop if it wasn't for that stupid thing,' Corbett glared at the Spellatron 3000, which continued to purr and display its little green light. 'It's made it all too easy. It's weird that her sister sent it. They don't get on, you know. Not in the habit of exchanging gifts.'

'I know. I thought that.'

'Well, I'm not getting roped in to help. I'm off home.'

'Bye, then,' said Elsie. 'Give my love to Crookfinger Forest.'

'Eh? You mean you don't know?'

'Know what?'

'The tower's not in the forest any more. She's moved it to Smallbridge Common.'

Chapter Four
A VERY LONG DAY

After nipping home to tell her surprised parents about their new neighbour, Elsie worked hard in Magenta's shop all day. It was her sort of thing, deciding where shelves should go, unpacking stock, arranging jars and stacking things in sensible places. Magenta was hopeless. She spent most of the time experimenting with the right sound for the shop bell. Or playing with the till.

Putting up shelves was easy. Elsie just told the Spellatron 3000 where they should go, the little green light blinked on and off and there they were on the walls. Instant shelving. No fuss.

Unpacking the boxes took a lot longer. Corbett started off not helping on principle, but finally relented, pecking the lids open and shouting out the contents. Elsie was grateful. Magenta had brought along the entire contents of her personal magic cupboards, as well as having done a mighty shop at the Sorcerer's Bazaar and ordering lots of fun-sounding stuff from the Jokus Pokus children's range in a magic catalogue. Elsie thought the Tickle Dust looked particularly intriguing. It came in a cute little golden pot with a red jewel on the lid, just the right size to fit into a small hand.

Finally, after long, back-breaking hours, just before sun set, it was done. Everything was in the right place, the floor was swept, the Spellatron 3000 had vanished the boxes – and the shop looked wonderful.

The stock consisted of the following:

1. Magenta's entire mail-order range: Squeeze 'n' Freezum Spray. Yes Drops. Belt-Up Balm, etc.

2. Every basic magical ingredient that all witches have in their cupboards, such as Moon Drops, Mustard Powder, Elf-Raising Flour, Tomato Catch-Up, Mermaid Breath, Dragon's Tears, Pickled Pepper, Strawberry Mint ... and much more.

 3. A range of cauldrons, from family-sized to single.

4. A clutch of broomsticks – more for the look of them than anything. Magenta didn't approve of broomsticks, but Elsie pointed out that a witches shop without broomsticks would be like a butcher's shop without sausages.

5. Pointy hats. Magenta had forgotten to buy any, so the Spellatron 3000 was called upon to provide a dozen. When they arrived – in a box, with a *whoosh*, if you're interested – they were all identical. Same shape, colour and size. Pointy, black, too small.

6. Two shiny kaftan-like gown things, one red with green dragons and one green with red

ones. Elsie draped them artistically over the dummies from the dump and added peacock feathers and necklaces of lucky horse shoes and Don't-Worry beads. The outfits looked rather good. They added glamour.

7. Bits and bobs, assorted: wands; magic mirrors; watches that told the time in seven dimensions; fake cobwebs to either wear like a shawl or just drape around the place; curly-toed slippers; safety gloves with reinforced fingertips, to be worn when throwing spells from a distance; genie lamps; turbans; wishing rings; wishbones; lucky charms; crystal balls; a couple of Hide-Me Hats, both in red.

8. The Jokus Pokus stuff for kids: Nevergon Sweets; Rainbow Bubblers; Musical Wands; Fizzy Wizzles; Hissy Wissies; Wiggly Spiders; Rubber fake snakes; and, of course, the pretty little pots of Tickle Dust.

'It looks good, doesn't it?' said Magenta as they both stood back and surveyed it. 'Didn't we do well? I'm exhausted. I'm off home for supper and an early night. Opening day tomorrow, need to get my strength up for the crowds. Lock up, Elsie, would you? Corbett, are you flying or coming with me?'

Corbett hopped onto her shoulder, and they instantly vanished, leaving Elsie to shut up shop.

When Elsie finally arrived home for supper, the boys were already in bed.

FAKE/SNAKES

★CRYSTAL BALLS★

TICKLE Dust

Musical Wands

'All ready for tomorrow?' asked Tilda, setting plates of stew on the table.

'Yes,' said Elsie. 'It's looking good. You must pop along and have a look, Mum.'

'I will. But I still don't understand why she's opened a magic shop here. There's no call for spells in Smallbridge, is there?'

'Magenta thinks Smallbridge needs shaking up. And that shop-keeping's easy. Just sitting down putting things in bags and taking the money.'

'Ha! I wish,' said Albert.

'Why *magical* stuff, though?' said Tilda. 'Isn't that a bit dangerous?' She glanced at Elsie. They didn't talk about it much, but Tilda knew her daughter had a knack for magic.

'Not if you follow the instructions, Mum,' said Elsie, reassuringly. 'It's like fireworks, or cooking. Be careful, no harm done.'

'Well, that's good to know,' said Tilda. 'Will a magic shop being so close to us affect our sales, do you think, Al?'

'I don't think so,' said Albert. 'We're selling very different things, aren't we? Whatever happens, I wish her success. We could do with a bit of variety in Smallbridge. We are a bit stuck in our ways here.'

To his surprise, Elsie leaned over and dropped a kiss on his head.

'What was that for?'

'For being a nice dad.'

Albert smiled. 'Well. I suppose you'll need to nip along and give her a hand tomorrow? Her being new to the business.'

'She says she's going to advertise for an assistant, but I think I might have to help her out in the meantime,' said Elsie, trying not to sound too excited. She didn't want to hurt her dad's feelings by appearing too keen. 'Sure you can spare me?'

'I'll manage,' Albert said.

'I took the boys along to have a look at the

tower on the common,' said Tilda. 'They loved it. They liked the flag at the top best. People say there's a rude bird that comes out, but it didn't when we were there.'

'That's Corbett,' said Elsie. 'He was helping set up the shop. What about you, Mum? Did *you* like the tower?'

'The ivy's pretty. I wouldn't like to live in it, mind, I'm no good with heights. There was a big crowd that had come to stare, so we couldn't get too near. But people did look a bit uneasy. I reckon they're nervous of coming face to face with your Witch Sharp, Elsie. She's got a reputation for having a short temper.'

'There's a public meeting tonight about our new arrival,' said Albert. He gave a little sigh. 'I'll go along. Show a bit of support for a fellow shopkeeper.'

'Can I come?' Elsie asked.

'No children allowed, pet.'

'Why not?'

'Because grown-ups think only grown-ups should make important decisions.'

'Well, that's silly,' said Elsie. 'I'm coming. I think Magenta needs *all* our help.'

Chapter Five
OUTRAGEOUS!

The council chamber was packed. Every chair was taken and people clustered in the doorway. News travelled fast in Smallbridge.

Albert and Elsie squeezed in at the back. Elsie had cast a little spell around herself so that no one noticed her. Not total vanishment like the Hide-Me hat, just a mild spell that made her instantly forgettable. People would look at her and immediately forget she was there. She had found out how to do it in one of the spell books she had borrowed from Magenta. It was the first time she had done it and it was working perfectly. Everyone just looked straight through her. Not her dad, though. He knew she was there.

From all around came a loud buzz of conversation. The Red Witch from Crookfinger Forest was opening a shop! Tomorrow morning! A shop selling spells! In Smallbridge! And if that wasn't enough, she'd gone and brought her accommodation with her! A thumping great tower, slap bang in the middle of the town common!

Everyone had plenty to say about the new shop – although nobody had actually *seen* it. In fact, the only information anyone had was from a couple of little kids called Eric and Thelma-Sue, who had been playing hide-and-seek around the dustbins and came racing back with

a hair-raising report:

There wuz a new magic shop where the dump used to be! It wuz, like, reeeeely red! There wuz all posters with writin'! There wuz big red twinklin' letters over the door! There wuz this 'orrible sound like a monster! That Red Witch lady came out so they runned away. No, they didn't stop to read the posters. Well, only one. One caught their eye. The one that said:

Neither Eric nor Thelma-Sue knew what Tickle Dust was, but they knew they wanted some.

The grown-ups had listened and absorbed

all this information with raised eyebrows, tight lips and snorts of disapproval. However, in Smallbridge, it didn't do to show too much interest right away. No one was prepared to be the first to gawp and get branded a nosy parker.

But the tower. Now, that was different. Everyone walked on Smallbridge Common on a Sunday so there wasn't a person present at the meeting who hadn't seen it. You certainly couldn't miss it. And no one could miss the talking bird who had appeared on the roof, told everyone to push off, then flown away, looking furious.

If truth be told, people felt a bit disappointed. Over the years there had been many rumours about the Moving Tower of Crookfinger Forest. That it was made of glass, or ice, or cheese, or something equally silly. The fact that it was made of plain grey stone was a bit of a let-down. It was big, granted, but essentially it was normal. There was even a privy round the back.

Anyway, all the adults agreed that whatever it looked like, it was taking up space on their common and was in clear breach of planning rules.

But, back now to the council chamber.

The meeting had been called by the mayor. His anxious little head poked up above the long table. Things were off to a bad start. There weren't enough chairs, and all but one of his councillors had called in sick, which always happened on public meetings.

'*Order!*' squeaked the mayor, banging his gavel. Nobody paid any attention.

The mayor's name was Sam Short. He lived with his mum. Annoyingly for him, he really was short. There is nothing wrong with that, but when he stood up to make speeches, he was often hard to see.

'*Order!*' he called again pathetically.

The man sitting next to him gave a sigh. This was Councillor Skinnard, the mayor's right-hand man. He had a long, pale face and a dry, dusty voice.

'Quiet, if you please,' ordered Councillor Skinnard. 'Settle down.'

Everyone settled down instantly. Those on chairs sat up properly. Those without chairs poked each other and stopped shuffling. Councillor Skinnard would have made a better mayor than Sam Short, but he preferred to be the power behind the throne. He had cleverly figured out that the blame always falls on the one *on* the throne, not the one behind it.

'So,' said Councillor Skinnard. 'This meeting has been called to address the business of two unlicensed buildings that have sprung up in Smallbridge overnight, both believed to be owned by the witch, Magenta Sharp. No booing, please, this isn't the playground. His Worship will now say a few words. The floor is yours, Mr Mayor.'

His Worship the mayor stood up to audible groans, sighs and restless muttering. Not everyone worshipped him.

'I know,' said Mayor Short. 'I *know* you're not happy. It's all very ... difficult. An uncomfortable situation.'

'It'd be comfier if we could sit down,' shouted a man at the back without a chair.

Elsie stifled a giggle.

'I only found out myself a short while ago,' explained the mayor. 'I believe one or two residents called earlier today to advise me of the prob— ah, the delicate situation. But I was mowing the lawn in the back garden all afternoon and didn't hear.'

There was a lot of scoffing at this. Everyone knew it was a lie. The mayor had been having a lie-in and told his mum not to answer the door.

'So now you've finally heard about it, what are you doing about it?' shouted a peevish voice that Elsie instantly recognized as belonging to Mr Sourman.

'I've had no time to do anything apart from call this meeting, sir,' said Mayor Short. 'But I intend to form a crisis committee to report back at the very earliest opportunity.'

'We don't need reports, we need *action!*' shouted a furious voice, coming from a man with a flat cap and a beard who was sitting in the middle of the front row. 'This is *outrageous!* A *witch* opening a *shop*! Selling bad, dangerous spells that *children* might get hold of!'

(Recognize him? He's the very same angry man who bought a hammer in the Emporium earlier on.)

'Right,' muttered voices. 'Health and safety!

Think of the kiddies!'

'That's not right,' Elsie whispered to Albert. 'Magenta doesn't sell bad spells, Dad. I should know. I unpacked it all.'

The angry beard man leaped to his feet and shook his fist in the air. 'And another thing!' he bellowed. 'She's got the cheek to park her ugly eyesore of a tower slap-bang in the middle of our common!'

There was vigorous clapping at this.

Albert stuck his hand up.

'Yes, Mr Pickles?' said the mayor. People quietened down. Albert had a calming influence. It was all those years of customer service.

'I would just like to point out that Witch Sharp's stock is most certainly not dangerous,' said Albert. 'In fact, it sounds rather entertaining. I have it on good authority that Witch Sharp is a *good* witch.'

'Is that so?' This was Mr Sourman again. 'And what authority would that be, Albert? Your Elsie, by any chance?'

'As for the tower on the common,' Albert continued, ignoring him, 'it's doing no harm.

There's plenty of space there.'

The crowd thought about this. Albert Pickles was well respected in the town. A man who usually talked good sense.

But—

'Witches can't be trusted, everyone knows

that,' bawled a woman in a green hat. 'Who does she think she is? Coming into our town, with her red gloves, starting a shop up at night, no warning, when decent folk are asleep. I hear it twinkles!'

'Before you know it, there'll be a whole row of twinkling witch shops selling rubbish on the high street!' shouted the man with no chair.

'Has she applied for planning permission?' enquired a man with a droopy moustache. 'That's what I'd like to know!'

'No,' said Councillor Skinnard. 'But all is in hand. His Worship intends to be there at the shop's opening first thing tomorrow morning.'

The mayor looked at him in alarm.

'You don't want to get off on the wrong foot, do you?' Councillor Skinnard murmured under his breath. 'Of course you must pay a visit. Do you want to appear witchist?'

'But I am,' said the mayor. 'Everyone here is. We don't like witches in Smallbridge.'

'But you don't want the *witch* to know that, do you?'

'Oh,' said the mayor. 'No. I see what you mean.'

'Dad,' hissed Elsie. 'This isn't fair. They want to shut her down before she's even open. What can we do?'

'Nothing right now, pet,' said Albert. He gave a sigh. 'I'm afraid it seems most minds are made up.'

'Oi! Mayor! Just to be clear,' shouted the man without a chair. 'First thing tomorrow you'll go and close her down, right?'

'Yes,' said the mayor. 'Most probably. Weather permitting.' Councillor Skinnard's sharp elbow dug into his side. 'I mean, rain or shine, I shall be there. I intend to be firm with the lady. Very firm indeed.'

'She should be thrown out of town! *Thrown! Hurled!*' The angry man with the beard was back again.

'Unbelievable,' remarked the woman with the green hat. 'Selling magic outright! Where anyone can walk in and buy some!'

'Well, *I* won't be buying anything, that's for certain,' said her friend, who had a single unbroken eyebrow. She gave a little shudder.

'Outrageous!' burst in angry beard man. 'No witch shops in Smallbridge!'

'Right!' roared the crowd.

'No witches in Smallbridge!' the beard cried again.

'No witches in Smallbridge!' the room echoed.

'Witches Unwelcome!'
'Witches Unwelcome!'
Albert and Elsie went home.

Chapter Six
OPENING DAY

The following morning, Mayor Short arrived in the alley at nine. He was clutching a briefcase containing planning application forms. In his head, he was rehearsing what he was going to say to the Red Witch. He would either start with, *'Now, see here, my good woman, this simply will not do!'* or, *'Charmed to meet you. I'm wondering if I can interest you in filling in a few forms?'* It depended on the level of threat when he arrived.

A sizeable crowd had also gathered at the

alley's entrance. People were very keen indeed to see how the mayor got on. A reporter from the newspaper was there, pad at the ready. The angry man with the beard was there (he gets everywhere, as you'll have noticed). So was the woman with the green hat and her friend with the eyebrow and the man with no chair. Mrs Lardy was there, and Mrs Snoring and Miss Winnie Whippet. And Mr Sourman.

Nobody had ventured down the alley.

The mayor himself wasn't at all keen on the task ahead. Nobody wants to confront a witch first thing in the morning.

The waiting crowd parted to let him through.

'Good morning,' he said. 'Lovely day for – um...' The rest of the sentence trailed away.

'Telling witches where to get off?' suggested a helpful voice from the crowd.

'Think you're up to the job, Mayor Short?' shouted the reporter. 'On a scale of one to ten, how nervous are you?'

The mayor pretended he hadn't heard.

Everyone watched him walk down the alley. Nuisance gave a friendly little tail wag as he approached the Emporium doorway. The mayor ignored him.

'Morning, Mr Mayor,' called Albert, who was giving the Emporium windows a fussy final polish.

'Good morning, Mr Pickles,' said the mayor unhappily. He walked on past, readying himself for the task ahead.

He had only just rounded the bend when Elsie appeared in the Emporium doorway. In her hand was a sausage.

'Here,' said Elsie, holding it out to Nuisance.

'Lovely breakfast for a good dog.' Nuisance downed it in one.

'The mayor's just gone by,' Albert told her.

'Ah. Right,' said Elsie. 'Perhaps I should pop along. Just to make sure things stay calm. Magenta's not too good with authority.'

'I suppose it wouldn't hurt,' said Albert. 'You need to teach her a bit of customer service, pet. You can't run a shop without it.'

'I'll just run in and take off my apron.'

'On the other hand, don't bother,' said Albert. 'He's already coming back.'

Both of them stared as the mayor came tottering unsteadily up the alley. His face was ghastly pale. There was a blankness about his gaze. No sign of the briefcase. Instead, a large toad was hopping along at his heels, its webbed feet leaving damp marks on the cobbles.

'All right, Mayor Short?' called Albert. 'Need to come in and sit down for a minute? Glass of water, perhaps?'

No response. The mayor tottered on, followed by the toad.

At the alley's entrance, the crowd parted once more to let him through. Nobody said anything. There was

something about the look of Mayor Short that made any comments or questions die in the throat. The toad didn't help. That was just … strange.

The mayor wobbled away down the main street and finally disappeared from view. So did the toad.

'Well,' said Mrs Lardy. 'I can't stop here all day. Need to pop into the Emporium for half a dozen screws and a new colander.'

The Emporium had never had such a busy morning. It seemed that everyone in Smallbridge had suddenly found themselves urgently in need of a kitchen mop, a packet of drawing pins or a wallpaper brush.

Elsie wanted to go and help Magenta, but there were so many customers there was no chance of slipping away. In fact, Elsie and Albert didn't have a moment's rest until the clock chimed midday and then, true to form, everyone disappeared for lunch.

'Well!' said Albert. 'That was unexpected. I even sold one of the green vases, did you notice?'

'I did. Now we've only got one hundred and seventy-nine left.'

Albert turned the sign on the door to CLOSED. 'Come on, pet, let's go up and get some lunch.'

'I think I'll just nip along and see Magenta,' said Elsie.

Magenta sat scowling behind the counter with her arms folded. The door opened and the shop bell jingled (Elsie had got her way with the bell).

'Hello,' said Elsie. 'How's it been going?'

'It's not,' snapped Magenta. 'No shortage of people standing and goggling, but not a single person came in, apart from that silly little mayor. Shouting some nonsense about planning permission, so I turned his briefcase into a toad. Rude little man.'

'I'm – um – not sure that's quite the right approach…'

'It's my approach and I'm not putting up with it. A shop is for selling things, not for being goggled at by people who have a sheep for a town statue. All I've done this morning is sit here and get *tutted* and *muttered* at from a distance. Somebody even threw an egg at the window. Of course, the window caught it and threw it back, and everyone ran off screaming. You'd think no one had ever seen magical self-defence glass before.'

'They haven't,' said Elsie. 'I told you, Smallbridge takes a while to get used to new things.'

'I can't wait for that. I'm not here to waste time. I'm here to get my specialist products back on the market. I shall spread the word. It's boring, sitting here on my own. No sign of Corbett. No loyalty whatsoever. By the way, I've written an advert for an assistant. As you claim you're not available.'

She pushed a piece of paper across the counter.

'"*Shop assistant wanted, apply Magenta Sharp, Sharp Spells, Smallbridge.*"' read Elsie. 'Well, it's brief and to the point. So where *is* Corbett?'

'Back at the tower. They're sulking together. They don't like it on that common. No trees. Too flat and open. And this morning there was a big crowd outside, just standing around gawping and making comments, watching me brush my teeth through the window. I really don't see what's so interesting.'

'They had a public meeting in the town hall last night,' said Elsie. 'About the tower and the shop. And you. Deciding what to do about everything.'

'Ah. That would explain the visit from that silly little mayor.'

'Dad did his best to stick up for you,' said Elsie. 'But an awful lot of people want you gone.'

'Too bad. I'm staying put. Oh, by the way, the till drawer's stuck. Fix it, would you?' Magenta looked around. 'Where did you put the box of disposable crystal balls?

'Over by the dummies. Next to the wands, by the fake spiders. Have you been forcing this drawer?'

'No.'

'It shouldn't stick, being new. What do you want a crystal for?'

'Because I'm going to drum up some business.'

'Right. Well, the drawer's working now. I could stay and help out for a bit if you like?'

'No point until we have customers,' said Magenta. Rummaging through the ball box.

'Oh. Okay, well I'll come back and see if you need help later, then?' said Elsie, feeling slightly disappointed to be returning to the Emporium quite so soon.

'Fine. Fine,' Magenta said with a dismissive wave of her hand.

Down beneath the counter, unnoticed at the back of a dark shelf, the Spellatron 3000 stopped purring for a split second – then resumed.

As Elsie left the shop, a tile slid off the roof and crashed to the cobbles.

She frowned down at the smashed tile. *Hmmm*, she thought. *That's not a good sign.*

★ ★ ★

The afternoon in the Emporium wasn't as hectic as the morning. The customers consisted of regulars, plus a few strays who hadn't yet seen Magenta's shop, and those who had come along for another look, just to be sure it was as bad as they remembered it. No one seemed in a hurry to leave. They had seen the tower and the shop and now they wanted to stand around and talk about them.

'Disgusting,' said Mr Sourman to Albert. He had come in to look at the cheap pens. He sucked noisily at his teeth.

'What is, Donald?' asked Albert politely.

'That witch shop.' He nodded over his shoulder. 'Disgusting. The colour, for a start.'

'I've never met Witch Sharp,' Mrs Snoring

mused. 'Not to speak to. I don't think I'd want to go in her shop.'

'Me neither,' said Mrs Lardy. 'I don't think we should encourage her. What if a bad spell gets in the wrong hands?'

Elsie gave a tired sigh. *Here we go again*, she thought.

'It won't,' she said. 'She doesn't sell bad spells.'

'What about the dear, innocent little ones, though?' said Miss Winnie Whippet, who didn't have any children. 'Suppose they get their darling, precious hands on something dangerous?'

'She doesn't *do* dangerous,' explained Elsie patiently. 'There's a whole, wonderful range of stuff, suitable for all the family.'

'Is that so?' said Mr Sourman. He sneered at Elsie. 'You think everyone should have access to magic, do you?'

'Actually, I do. Magic is perfectly safe if you follow the instructions.'

'And you would know, of course.' Mr Sourman gave Elsie a knowing stare. 'Being so pally with her.'

'Are you buying that pen, Donald?' asked Albert. He sounded chilly. 'Shall I put it in a bag for you?'

Mr Sourman ignored him. His mean little eyes were fixed on Elsie.

'She's taught you a few little tricks of your own, am I right?'

Here it is, then, thought Elsie. *The storm in the teacup.* She had known it would come up one day.

More people had come into the shop now and were listening while pretending not to. The angry man with the flat cap and the beard was among them, stamping around giving angry little snorts because he couldn't see what he wanted (thick black chalk to make an angry poster).

'Are you actually planning to *buy* anything today, Donald?' asked Albert.

'Well, Albert, I'm not sure if this is the kind of establishment I want to spend my money in,' said Mr Sourman. 'What with that girl of yours liking a little magical dabble. Tell your dad what I caught you doing with the tea. Go on, missy!'

There was an audible gasp. Nobody talked to Elsie Pickles like that. She was always so nice. So polite and helpful. Whatever did he mean by it?

'Donald,' said Albert coldly. 'I'll thank you

not to speak to Elsie like that.'

Albert was a mild-mannered man who rarely raised his voice. But every now and then, he exploded. You always knew when he was rising to the boil because his nose would twitch. It was twitching now.

'Never mind, Dad,' said Elsie. 'It's fine.'

'I'm speaking my mind,' said Mr Sourman. 'You're too soft, Albert. Letting your daughter go running off into the forest, learning how to do bad spells, mixing with the wrong crowd.'

'Quite right!' suddenly chipped in angry beard man. 'What's Smallbridge coming to? Witches opening shops! Towers appearing overnight! Shop keepers letting their kids run wild. Outrageous!'

Well. That's how it began.

Albert, as we know, is a stickler for good

customer service. But that afternoon he broke one of his own rules. Rule Eighteen. Do Not Get Into Arguments With Customers.

He broke that one in a *big* way.

Chapter Seven
THREE WITCHES

The following morning, three new witches arrived in Smallbridge.

The trio marched purposefully up the high street, all armed with large shopping baskets, one of which was on wheels and contained a large yellow teapot. Elsie, had she been there, would have recognised them immediately. Wendy Snipe, the Wise Woman of Clackham Common; Maureen, the Hag of Heaving Heath and Madame Shirley, Fortune Teller to the Stars. Elsie had met them in the

Sorcerer's Bazaar.

Wendy was the plump one with the grey curls and beaming smile. Maureen was thin and mournful with the traditional black robes. Tiny Shirley was dressed like some sort of mad clown and went nowhere without her teapot.

The residents of Smallbridge were once again taken by surprise. Witch sightings in Smallbridge were rare. Certainly not three at a time. People's jaws dropped open. People whispered. People nudged each other. Some of the ruder ones pointed.

The children were hugely excited. A magic shop, a tower with a rude raven, something called Tickle Dust and now more witches! This was the best week ever! It certainly beat climbing on the sheep.

As the three witches paraded down the

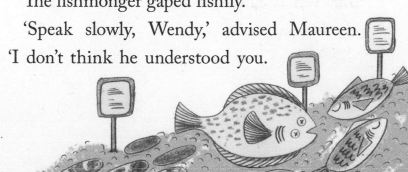

street, there came the hasty pulling-down of shutters and the slamming of doors. Of the shopkeepers, only two stayed outside. One was the fishmonger. He had wanted to go in, but at the sight of three witches, his legs had gone wobbly and wouldn't obey him. So he just stood stock still, giving a rather good impression of one of his fish – mouth agape and eyes staring. The other was the greengrocer, who continued to set out his apple display. He wasn't from Smallbridge and he wasn't witchist.

'Is this the right way to Sharp Spells, lovie?' Wendy enquired of the fishmonger. 'Nice-looking fish you got there, I might pop in later.'

The fishmonger gaped fishily.

'Speak slowly, Wendy,' advised Maureen. 'I don't think he understood you.

Maybe the poor fellow's hard of hearing?'

Wendy raised her voice and spoke in crisp, clear tones. 'WE ARE LOOKING FOR A SHOP CALLED SHARP SPELLS! ARE WE HEADING THE RIGHT WAY?'

'It's down the alley on your right, ladies,' said the greengrocer helpfully. 'Had breakfast, have you? You know what they say about apples being good for you.'

'Thank you, young man,' said Wendy. 'What's wrong with him?' She pointed at the fishmonger. 'Shark got his tongue?'

'Just a bit shy. We don't see many witch ladies like yourselves in Smallbridge. More's the pity.'

'Flatterer,' said Shirley. 'I'll think I *will* have a bag of those delicious-looking apples.'

★ ★ ★

Elsie and Albert leaned on the counter next to each other. Both of them felt a bit down in the dumps. They were open and ready for business as usual. But the shop was deserted.

'It's early yet, Dad,' said Elsie, as the clock ticked. She moved to the window and stared out.

'Mm.' Albert sounded worried.

'Someone's sure to come in.'

'Mm.'

'Here comes someone now— *Oh! Oh my!*'

'What's wrong, love?'

'Three witches just walked by! I know them!'

'You do? How's that, then?'

'I ... met them in a ... shop,' said Elsie vaguely. She tended not to talk much about magical things around the family. It made all of them a little bit uncomfortable. 'Magenta went to school with them. It looks like whatever she did to draw in customers is working'

'She's lucky,' said Albert glumly. 'I've a feeling we won't get anyone in today. Not after yesterday's … incident.'

The 'incident' had involved loud voices and shouted accusations and people taking sides. There had been pushing and shoving and fist waving. Toes were trodden on. Miss Winnie got one of her headaches. It wasn't what you expected when you went to buy a stamp.

At one point during the scuffle, a lemon squeezer fell out of Mr Sourman's overcoat pocket, along with a tube of glue and a box of matches, none of which had been paid for. That was the thing that really did it for Albert. He had thrown both Mr Sourman and angry beard man out of the shop. Instead of a nice shop, the Emporium had become a nasty shop where there were fights. A shop to be avoided.

'Sorry, Elsie, love,' said Albert. 'I can't believe I did that. It went against every customer service rule there is. I've given the Emporium a bad reputation.'

'You were standing up for me! And I'm pleased that you did, so thank you, Dad,' said Elsie. 'Cheer up. They'll be back when they need a sink plunger or a bar of soap.'

She hoped she was right.

'I'm trying, pet,' said Albert. 'But sometimes I get tired of Smallbridge. Don't get me wrong, I love the Emporium. But occasionally I think about living somewhere completely different. Where people – I don't know – smile a bit more.'

Elsie had never thought that her dad might feel that way. The shop was his world and she always thought he loved living in Smallbridge. But she also knew how much she loved staying in the forest with Magenta, seeing completely different things and meeting new people. Elsie couldn't remember her parents ever even having a holiday, so it wasn't really surprising Albert might get a bit fed up with the same old routine.

She wandered across to the doorway and gave a little sigh. Albert came out to join her. He put an arm around Elsie's shoulders. Nuisance crept up with an old shoe he'd been saving. It was all a bit depressing.

And then, suddenly, Joey arrived and everyone cheered up!

Inside Sharp Spells, Magenta's first three

customers were inspecting the merchandise. They picked things up, shook things and sniffed things, throwing them back any old where, which is the way that witches like to shop. Magenta stood erect behind the counter, trying to look and act like Elsie. Relaxed. Welcoming. Helpful. It didn't come naturally.

'Well,' said Wendy. 'You *have* done a nice job and no mistake, Madge. 'Very nice little shop.'

'Yes,' said Magenta. 'I know. Don't wave the wands about, Wendy, they've only got a small amount of power.'

'And you did it all by yourself, you say?'

'Yes. Put the wand down.'

'Must have taken a bit of doing. Getting a whole shop up and running overnight.'

'It did. Put it *down*.'

Shirley was fingering the beautifully-draped

red kimono which slipped to one side of the dummy, quite spoiling the effect. The string of No Worries Beads came undone and fell on the floor.

'If that's broken, you have to pay for it,' said Magenta.

'A bit too much red, if you don't mind my saying so,' went on Wendy. 'I know it's your signature colour, dear, but I'd tone it down a bit. Or sell dark glasses. And you don't need quite so many posters. And I'd turn off the twinkling letters. They're wasted in a dreary town like this.'

'Actually,' said Shirley, 'All the S's have stopped twinkling. It reads *Harp Pell the Hop*. I noticed earlier.'

'Really?' Magenta frowned. 'That shouldn't happen.'

'The floor dips a bit here and there too,' said Shirley. 'Feels a bit – insubstantial. Like you could put your foot through it. And the roof's missing a couple of tiles.'

'It sounds as though you don't like anything about my shop,' said Magenta, sounding a bit sulky.

'Oh, no, dear, we *do*,' said Shirley. 'I don't think I know of any witches who've opened a shop. You're a trail blazer. We're just surprised you didn't mention what you were planning.'

'Why should I?' said Magenta. 'What do you expect me to do, call you every day to discuss my business plans?'

'It's well stocked, I have to say,' said Maureen, who was over in the children's corner trying out Fizzy Wizzles (little green sparklers that burned, fizzed out and finally turned into peppermint gum you could chew). 'Good idea to sell the basics as well as your own spells. That'll save me having to drag off to the Sorcerer's Bazaar every time I run out of dried newt spit. I see you have it in three flavours. Can't say I fancy pineapple.'

'I'm surprised young Elsie hasn't helped you out,' asked Wendy, picking up a red Hide-Me Hat, putting it on and disappearing. 'Nice and nearby, isn't she? We just passed by her dad's shop. But you did it all on your own, you say?'

'Mmm,' said Magenta. 'Take off that hat unless you're buying it, Wendy, I've asked you not to handle the merchandise. I hope you're going to pay for those sweets, Maureen.'

Wendy reappeared and dropped the hat on the floor. 'How much are those bats on elastic? I'm thinking of my grandson.'

'He'd sooner have one of these, I reckon,' said

Shirley, picking up a little gold pot of Tickle Dust and examining it. 'There's a red jewel on the lid. What kiddy wouldn't want that?' She turned it upside down and read the instructions out loud: "*A pinch down the neck and you'll giggle like heck! Hand crushed by jolly elves. Under-fives use with supervision.*" Sounds like a laugh. How much is this, Madge?'

'I have no idea, look at the label. Look, are any of you going to buy anything or are you just going to stand round eating and fiddling with things?'

'There's one thing you can't get in this shop and that's a cup of tea,' said Wendy. 'It's a shame you didn't think of that, Madge. A café would be lovely. Somewhere to sit and go through what you just bought over a cuppa tea. Right, Shirley?'

Elsie and Joey stood in a shaft of morning sunlight outside the empty Emporium. Bill the basket sat quietly on the cobbles at Joey's feet. Nuisance was dabbing it with his paw, hoping it would play. But Bill was playing by Smallbridge rules. No floating in public.

Albert, having given up on any customers appearing, had gone upstairs to have a cuppa with Tilda and play with the boys – something he rarely had time to do.

'She's opened a *magic shop*?" said Joey.

'Yep. Just round the bend, where the dump was.'

'Great! Good use of space!'

'She's not making herself popular. She turned the mayor's briefcase into a toad.'

'Oh,' said Joey. 'Not so great.'

'And she's moved the tower to Smallbridge Common.'

'*What?*'

'You heard. The tower's on the common, causing a huge amount of drama.'

'She never told me. I'm the post boy, I'm supposed to know when people move address. What does Corbs make of all this?'

'He hates it. Crowds of people coming to stare all day. The tower's not happy either. But Magenta says she wants it there so she can get to the shop easily. Claims she's going to walk there and back for exercise.'

'She won't,' said Joey. 'She'll take shortcuts. I'm surprised she even put in the hard work to open a shop at all.'

'She didn't. Her sister sent her some weird

new gadget that did it all for her.' said Elsie. 'Corbett and I don't trust it. It didn't come with proper instructions.'

'Hmmm. What's it like? The magic shop?'

'Flashy outside, and packed with great stuff inside, but it just doesn't … feel right somehow, but I can't put my finger on what's wrong with it.'

Joey nodded. 'Sounds a bit fishy,' He reached into his pocket and pulled out an envelope. 'I've got a letter for Her Witchiness so I'll pop along and see the shop for myself. Nuisance can run to the tower and fetch Corbs and then I'll come back and the five of us can discuss what's what.'

'You mean four,' said Elsie. 'Me, you, Nuisance and Corbett.'

'You forgot Bill.'

'Oh, yes. Sorry. Look, *I'll* get Corbett. See

you back here in ten minutes.'

And before Joey could remind her about cutting down on shortcuts, she was gone.

Instantly, Elsie was in the tower kitchen! It was really exhilarating. Elsie had missed taking shortcuts. All the time they saved. The fun of them!

She felt at home right away. The tower was glad to see her too. The minute she arrived, she could feel it perk up a bit. But it still felt a bit out of sorts. Unsettled. Obviously unhappy on a dull, draughty common with no sheltering trees, too much sky and a constant crowd of onlookers.

Elsie peeked out of the curtains at the crowd.

Somebody shouted,
'Oi! Where's the rude
bird?' She snapped the
curtains shut again.

'Hello, Tower,'
she said. 'It's
good to be
back. Sorry
I haven't been
along to see
you. I'm told
you don't
much like it
here.'

The tower gave a little shiver. Somewhere upstairs, a door banged. A small jug fell off a hook and broke on the floor. The tap went on and off by itself, just a small, disgusted squirt. No. It didn't like it.

'What d'you want, Elsie?' came a cross croak from Corbett's sleeping perch. 'May pelicans peck your pimply ears, be quiet. I'm *trying* to catch forty winks here. I've been up on the roof screaming at sightseers since sun up.'

'Joey's back at the Emporium. Are you coming?'

'Really? Oh! Good. Yep, right away.' Corbett perked up immediately and flapped on to her shoulder. 'What are we waiting for, take a shortcut, let's go!'

Wendy, Maureen and Shirley stepped out of Sharp Spells, their baskets full to overflowing. All three had the triumphant look that people get when they've experienced the perfect shopping trip. A trip where they found absolutely everything they wanted, plus some extra treats.

Behind them, the door slammed shut, causing a sudden shower of red paint. Another tile fell off the roof.

'Some good stuff she's got in there,' said Maureen. 'Credit where it's due.'

'I don't believe she set that shop up all by herself, though,' said Shirley. 'Not for a minute. She's taken a shortcut. I hear there's some sort of newfangled gadget out. Cuts your time right down. Uses a different sort of magic.'

'I don't trust new sorts of magic,' said Wendy. 'You don't know what they put in it.'

'Oh, here's Pickles' Emporium, little Elsie's dad's place,' said Shirley. 'Shall we pop in and say hello, as we're in the neighbourhood?'

'Could do' said Maureen. 'Looks like the sort of useful shop that just might have clothes pegs.'

'They do! I can see 'em,' said Wendy, peering into the Emporium window. 'Ooh. I don't know about you two, but I *love* them green glass vases!'

In Sharp Spells, Joey was walking around with

his mouth open, Bill bobbing happily in his wake. This was a magic shop, where a floating basket was free to be itself.

'This is great!' said Joey, meaning it. There was nothing he loved more than a magic shop. 'I could spend hours here. Bill and I are coming back on Thursday. It's our day off.'

'Right,' said Magenta shortly. 'Thanks.'

'They bought a lot, didn't they? Your first three customers? I saw their baskets.'

'They did,' said Magenta 'I didn't enjoy it much, though. I'm exhausted with all that trying to be nice. Shop work's not as easy as you think. I've advertised for an assistant. You wouldn't be interested, would you?'

'Yes! Yes! Yes, I would!' cried Joey, the mad-for-magic boy.

'On second thoughts, forget it. I need someone

with the knack, like Elsie. Not just nice, like you. No offence.'

'None taken, I suppose,' said Joey. He gave a small sigh. Bill the basket gave him a comforting little nudge. At least he was nice. 'I've got a job anyway.'

'There's another thing bothering me a bit,' went on Magenta. 'I haven't mentioned it because Corbett will only say he told me so, but I've noticed a few faults with the shop. Cracks have appeared in the walls. The till keeps sticking. And the outside S's have lost their twinkles. Plus the posters are drooping and the roof's losing tiles. It's not quite as perfect as it was in the beginning.'

'Can't you fix it?'

'I don't know how,' admitted Magenta. Her eyes flicked below the counter, where the Spellatron 3000 sat back in the shadows, purring. Except … the purr didn't sound quite as convincing as before. There was a rusty quality to the sound. And when the little green light blinked out, it took longer to come back on again.

'Look on the bright side,' said Joey. 'Your friends showed up and bought loads. Tomorrow, you won't move for customers. You should celebrate tonight. Ask the tower for a cake. I'll come round.'

'The tower's sulking. No cakes. But you're right. I should look on the bright side. After all, it is early days.'

'By the way, I've got a letter for you,' said Joey, reaching into his sack. 'From your sister, by the looks of the writing.'

'Put it under the till,' said Magenta. 'Her

letters are always so depressing. I'm sure it's nothing important anyway.'

Chapter Eight
SYLPHINE

The following day passed into Smallbridge legend as The Day the Witches Came. Because come they did. By broomstick, by bicycle, on foot, but mostly by shortcut. By nine o'clock in the morning, a long queue of them snaked along the alley, spilling out into the high street. Smallbridge didn't know what to do about this. Everyone thought that the mayor should deal with it, but he wasn't answering the door again. Albert, Elsie and Corbett watched the queue through the Emporium window. Corbett had come on a flying visit as a break from shouting insults. As he explained, he needed to rest his throat now and then. He was becoming quite a celebrity. He was known as the 'funny bird on the roof'. Children kept pestering their parents to go and see him.

The witches came in all shapes and sizes. Some looked cheerful and expectant. Some looked fierce and determined. Some chattered to their neighbours, some didn't. Some were all dressed up, and some were a total mess and clearly didn't care. All were armed with a variety of serious-looking shopping bags.

Mixed in with them, to Elsie's surprise, were a few Smallbridge parents with excited children hanging off them. It seemed that not everyone in Smallbridge was witchist (though you wouldn't know it from the town meeting). There were quite a few who were intrigued by the idea of a magic shop. The children were proving popular with the witches, who patted them on the head, chucked their chins and told them they were clever. (They were certainly clever at pestering their parents for Tickle Dust which had now reached mythic status although no one actually knew what it was.)

'Looks like Wendy and her friends have spread the word,' said Corbett. 'The crystal balls must have been hot last night.'

'Where do they all come from?' gasped Albert.

'All over,' said Elsie. 'They look really out of place in Smallbridge, don't they?'

'But they are potential customers,' said Albert, finally pulling himself together and closing his mouth. 'I'm sure they're the same as anyone

once when you get to know them. A few more warts and broomsticks, maybe, but nothing wrong with that. We could certainly do with a few more like your three friends yesterday, pet.'

The day before had turned out to be a good one after all. Wendy, Maureen and Shirley had indeed descended upon the Emporium. And once Elsie had been hugged and kissed with huge enthusiasm, the three of them had then proceeded to shop.

A witch's shopping basket is never full, however highly heaped. The three witches bought clothes pegs, nails, pens, dish mops, scissors, door mats, hair nets, kettles, ironing boards and many more dull but necessary items. All three bought a green vase. In fact, Wendy bought two. One for herself and one for her sister (which she said she'd have back if her own got broken). Elsie had been relieved to serve customers again. It felt like the Emporium was once again back on track.

But that was yesterday. Today, it seemed nobody was interested in the Emporium. The waiting witches were there for one thing only: *Sharp Spells The Shop!*

The clock on the town hall struck nine. Opening time. The queue shuffled forward.

'Do you want to pop along and give her a hand, pet?' asked Albert. 'It looks like another quiet morning for us. Unless you think she'll cope on her own.'

'She won't,' said Corbett. 'She'll already be on the point of jacking it in.'

He was right. When Elsie arrived, squeezing past the queue, saying things like, 'I'm sorry,' and, 'Excuse me, can I get past, please?' she found Magenta sitting bolt upright at the till with her arms crossed. The shop was packed. From the doorway came impatient grumbling and the odd cry of 'Hurry up, don't have all day!' Magenta looked as though for two pins she'd freeze the lot of them and take a shortcut home.

'The drawer's stuck again,' she growled and then looked at Elsie a bit sheepishly. 'Actually, a few funny things are happening.'

'I was worried something wasn't right,' said Elsie. 'It's the Spellatron 3000, isn't it? There's something funny about its magic. It seems to be losing power.'

'Have a look at it, will you?' said Magenta. 'Be quick. I don't want anyone knowing about it.'

Elsie dipped her head under the counter. 'It's

not purring as steadily. More like a weak sort of gaspy noise. And the blinking green light's slowed down. It's hardly flashing at all.'

'How much are the Yes Drops, miss?' demanded a customer.

'Be quiet,' snapped Magenta. 'Can't you see we're talking?'

'One shilling. Two bottles for the price of one, a bargain,' said Elsie pleasantly. 'How many would you like, madam?'

Once she'd dealt with that customer, there was another close behind and then another, and soon Elsie found herself a permanent fixture behind the counter, serving customers with a smile.

Every so often she would look up and notice another defect in the shop, items tumbling off shelves, a table wobbling and falling over, a tin popping open. But even as she worried about the Spellatron 3000's failing magic, she felt in her element behind the counter. She would never admit it to her dad, but it was more fun working in a shop that sold spells rather than screws. The customers were different too. They liked to poke things and smell things and try things out. There were pink sparks and rains of little blue stars. Things fizzled and twinkled and went off with a bang. There were strange smells.

Corbett helped put things in bags and even worked the till, pecking the keys with his beak. The children were delighted to get a chance to see the 'rude bird' up close, but even Corbett wasn't as big a hit as the Tickle Dust. The little gold pots were eagerly clutched in hot little hands to be tried out later, under the supervision of an adult, as instructed on the bottom.

Magenta slumped in the chair behind the counter, reading *Witch!* magazine and eating her way through a bag of Nevergon biscuits from the children's range. When witches complimented her on the new shop, she gave a surly shrug and carried on reading. Everything else was left to Elsie.

Elsie didn't mind, though. She was having a lovely time.

And there we shall leave them for now – because someone else needs our attention.

Back in the Emporium, Albert was on his own, wondering whether to give up and close for the day, when the door burst open. A girl in an unflattering navy blue suit staggered in backwards, arms wheeling wildly, and crashed into the stack of green vases, which toppled noisily to the floor. Rather to Albert's disappointment, none of them smashed.

'Oops,' said the girl. 'Sorry. I'll pick them up.'

'Don't worry, young lady,' said Albert. 'I'm thinking of discontinuing the line anyway.'

'I got jostled,' said the girl, climbing to her feet. 'It's mad out there. These stupid shoes don't help.' She glared down at her feet, which sported a pair of ugly, thick-soled shoes. 'It's like having boulders strapped on. Are you Mr Pickles?'

'I am,' said Albert. 'And you are?'

'Sylphine Greenmantle.'

Ah-ha, thought Albert. *Elsie's friend from the forest.*

He tried remembering what Elsie had said about her. Something about dressing like a wood sprite. Long hair with flowers in, wafty gowns, that sort of thing.

But that didn't sound a bit like the girl in front of him. This girl was all bundled up in a thick, scratchy-looking suit and wore shoes like bricks. Her hair was scraped back into a bun. Not a flower in sight.

Albert quickly applied Customer Service Rule Eleven: Never Show Surprise.

'Well, I'm very pleased to meet you, Sylphine. What an … unusual name.'

'I know. I like it too. But Granny says I should use my real name, Aggie Wiggins, when I'm interviewed for the job because Witch Sharp will have no time for nonsense, she says. Granny says I'm not to mention moon dancing or talk about animals.'

'You're … after the shop assistant job?'

'Yes. Granny saw the advert on a tree. She says even shop work is preferable to moonlight dancing. I was hoping Elsie would give me some tips. Where is she?'

'Helping Witch Sharp out. Business is brisk, as you can see from the queue.'

They both looked out of the window. The queue was moving, but didn't seem to be getting any shorter. Every time it looked like it was shrinking, a whole new crowd of customers would join at the back.

'So you've got no one to help you when a customer comes in here?' said Sylphine.

'I don't think that's very likely,' said Albert. 'It's a slow day.'

'But if one should.'

'One won't,' sighed Albert. 'We had a flurry of customers yesterday, but it's all gone quiet again—'

Right on cue, the bell jangled and, suddenly, two witches were in the shop. One was short and round and wore half-glasses. The other was dressed in purple, and had an eye patch. Both of their shopping baskets were heaped with products from Sharp Spells. Bottles rattled, fake snakes for the grandkids wiggled, and now and again in from the depths of the bags there would come a small, muffled explosion or a burst of green sparkles as magical artefacts rubbed up against each other. Glinting on the top of both baskets were pretty little gold pots with red jewels in the lids.

'Why, ladies,' smiled Albert. 'Can I be of service? Or shall I let you look around and see if anything catches your eye?'

'We want one of these green vases you sold Wendy Snipe yesterday,' said the short, round witch. She nudged one with her foot. 'Hmmm. Funny place to display 'em, on the floor.'

'Don't worry, Mr Pickles,' said Sylphine. 'I'll

pick them up. I'll help you. Then I can say I've had work experience in a shop when I go for my interview.'

'I really don't need any help—' began Albert, but broke off because the shop bell announced the arrival of yet more witch customers. All of them had clearly enjoyed shopping in Sharp Spells – the evidence was the full to bursting shopping bags – but the day was young and there was no hurry to get home. Might as well check out the shop next door.

And after that – well, it wasn't often you bumped into old what's her name from wherever. Wouldn't hurt to stop for a natter and a catch-up. Buy a fish for supper, perhaps. Take a stroll around the town, see what it had to offer. It didn't look promising, but you never knew. Maybe there would be a café.

For the rest of that day, Albert sold a very respectable load of stuff, all to a steady stream of witches on their way back from Sharp Spells. The hideous green vases were a surprise hit. Matches were popular. As one witch explained to him, they were always blowing out when you're trying to get a fire going on a blasted heath on a windy night, so you could never have too many. And it was surprising how many witches couldn't resist a chicken tea towel.

All this and more Albert sold, always at his most charming, never slipping up once on customer service, despite being driven to distraction by Sylphine, who, unsurprisingly, turned out to be the worst shop assistant in the world.

The Pickles family talked about it that night, as they cleared away the supper dishes, keeping their voices low because Sylphine was at that moment flat out and snoring on the sofa, still wearing her awful suit and shoes. She'd arrived in Smallbridge without thinking about where she would stay or how she would eat. She had also forgotten to bring any money. The choice for the Pickles was simple: either they offered her the sofa, or she would be sleeping in the doorway with Nuisance.

Elsie washed, Tilda dried and Albert wiped

down the table.

'She's hopeless,' whispered Albert to Tilda and Elsie. 'I've never known anyone so clumsy. What shall we do with her?'

'I don't know,' said Elsie, trying to hold in a yawn. She was ready for bed.

'She kept saying "*I'll do that*" and I'd say "*no, don't*",' Albert went on, 'and then she did it anyway, all wrong. Three times she stacked the special offer ironing boards. Three times they fell over again. Onto customers.'

'Oh, dear.'

'She got her hair caught in the till. Your mum had to come down and untangle it. She knocks things off shelves, drops things, gives the wrong change...'

'She ate a good supper, though,' said Tilda. 'Likes her food, I'll say that. And she was ever so pleased to see *you*, Elsie.'

'She was,' said Elsie with a smile. Her arms still felt sore from Sylphine's enthusiastic hugs of joy when she had finally arrived back at the attic (on foot, although she had been sorely tempted to take a shortcut) well after closing time.

'It's been a funny old day,' mused Albert.

'I took the boys to the common to look at the tower at sunset and see if the rude raven was there,' said Tilda. 'I got the sense that people are coming around to the idea of the tower being in Smallbridge. Everyone seemed a lot more friendly.'

'Really?' said Elsie.

'Yes. And I don't know how, but suddenly there are benches in the square and a pretty fountain in the middle,' said Tilda. 'The boys said the water tastes like lemonade, of all things! And there were a load of witches sitting around, showing each other what they'd been buying. A couple of them were using the sheep to barbecue on.'

'Best thing for it,' said Albert.

'Really nice, they were. They gave the boys a free sausage. Arthy especially was a real hit with the witches. He sang "Twinkle Twinkle" and got given a little gold pot with a jewel on the lid.'

'Tickle Dust,' said Elsie. 'All the kids are after that. It's very popular in Sharp Spells.'

'Arthy couldn't get the lid off.'

'It's a safety thing. What do the witches make of Smallbridge?'

'There were complaints about the shops being closed and there being nothing to do and nowhere to sit and nowhere to get a cup of tea. Asked me what we do for fun around here. I said nothing really. Apart from the farmer's market tomorrow.'

'They'll have all moved on by morning, I bet,' said Albert. 'Stocked up on magic and the best the Emporium can offer. There's nothing here to keep their interest. It's a shame really because we had a great day today. What will happen then is anyone's guess. Especially if the regulars don't come back.'

'Actually,' said Tilda, 'I kind of hope they don't move on. They've certainly livened things up a bit.'

Tired though Elsie was, before she went to bed, she took a shortcut along to the square. She popped up next to the sheep which was indeed being used as a barbecue by Wendy, Shirley and Maureen. Nuisance was sitting nearby, hoping for a sausage.

'Hello, dear,' said Shirley. 'Corn on the cob? Bag of chestnuts?'

'I've had supper, thanks,' said Elsie. 'I just popped along to see how things are going.'

She looked around. There was a full moon shining. The square was full of locals and witches

alike. Somebody was playing an accordion. The fountain was fizzing and people were collecting free lemonade in bottles. There was a nice, festive atmosphere.

What a difference a day made.

Chapter Nine
THE MARKET!

The following morning, Elsie and Joey bumped into each other in the middle of the high street. Elsie had the three boys with her, plus Nuisance. Joey had Bill.

'Hi, where are you going?' Elsie and Joey said at the same time, and giggled.

'We're off to the market,' said Elsie. 'I'm buying the boys toffee apples.'

'Bill and me are off to Sharp Spells,' said Joey happily.

His pockets jingled with the contents of his

piggy bank. His plan was to fill Bill to the brim with tricks and fireworks and anything going that was cheap, noisy or sparkly.

'I wouldn't rush,' said Elsie. 'It's not open. Yesterday was all too much for Magenta.'

'Yep!' croaked a voice from above. 'Still in bed, snoring.' There was a feathery flurry, and Corbett landed on Elsie's shoulder. 'Me? I've been up for hours. Early bird catches the small, dry, rubbish worms that crawl around that awful common. No one's got a sandwich, by any chance?'

'Couldn't you get something from the magic larder?' asked Elsie.

'The tower's still on strike.' Corbett eyed Arthy, Toby and Baby Todd, who stood holding hands in a row, wide-eyed and thrilled beyond belief to see the rude raven up close. 'What are those?'

'My little brothers,' said Elsie. 'We're off to the market for toffee apples. Say hello to Joey and Corbett, boys.'

'Heddo,' said Arthy shyly.

'Ho,' said Toby, even shyer.

Baby Todd just sucked his thumb.

'Toffee apples, eh?' said Corbett. 'I'd have one with you, but they glue up my beak.' He crossed his eyes and made funny glued-up beak motions, which sent all three boys into convulsions of laughter. 'See that? Little kids love me.'

'Well,' said Elsie, 'we'd best be going—'

'I got tickoduss,' announced Arthy suddenly, eager to impress the funny-talking bird and the big boy. He reached into his pocket and produced the little gold pot with a red jewel in the lid.

'Wow!' cried Joey. 'Great name, great pot, got to be great stuff. Let's try it.'

'Not now,' said Elsie. 'We need to get to the toffee apple stall before they sell out.'

'Come on, let's try it now. Look how cute it is. If it's any good, I'll buy some. Arthy wants to try it, don't you, Arthy?'

'Eth.'

'Corbs wants to, don't you, Corbs? Come on, back me up here.'

'Market first,' said Elsie firmly. 'I promised the boys a treat because they've been good. They sat and watched Sylphine finish off their favourite breakfast cereal and nobody cried.'

'Aggie's here?' said Joey.

'She turned up yesterday and helped out in the Emporium … well, sort of.'

'Why would Aggie help in your dad's shop?'

asked Joey.

'Her granny wants her to be Magenta's assistant and Sylphine thought working at the the Emporium would be good experience. She's going to see Magenta this morning to ask for the job.'

Oooooooowwwwwww!

Everyone jumped at the odd howl that suddenly echoed in the morning air.

Ooooooooooowwww!

Another. Coming from the direction of the town square.

Arthy, Toby and Baby Todd grabbed Elsie's skirt. Nuisance went stiff and growled. Elsie, Corbett and Joey stared at each other. They knew those howls.

'The Howlers.' said Elsie. 'Whatever are they doing in Smallbridge?'

'Let's find out,' said Joey.

The Farmers' Market was the highlight of Smallbridge's week. You could buy most things there: vegetables, cheese, honey and eggs. There was a woman who sold toffee apples, a man who sold cheap shoes and a knife grinder.

The market was always busy, but today it wasn't just the locals hustling and bustling, there were plenty of witches too, filling their baskets with turnips, cabbages, horrible pairs of slippers and dangerously sharp kitchen knives. But rather than it being confrontational, there was lots of polite head nodding and the occasional, 'Excuse me,' and, 'after you.' Elsie was delighted to see everyone getting along.

As the group made their way through the crowd, Elsie spotted the Howler sisters staked out in a corner spot. Two smiling little old ladies, one in pink, one in blue, both with matching bonnets and parasols – and each with a tail sticking through a special slot at the back of their dresses. It was very strange to see them

in Smallbridge.

Behind them was a row of buckets. Planted in each was a tall, stiff, green stalk topped with a large, white, round flower that … glowed. Gave out weird, silvery light. Smelled odd too. Sweet. Tangy. Like nothing else on earth.

A sign next to the buckets said:

MOONFLOWERS
NEED GOOD HOMES

'Why, if it isn't Elsie and the post boy!' cried Evie (in pink). 'Give a good home to a moonflower, dears?'

'Lovely, aren't they?' said Ada (in blue). 'We grow them from seed. Don't need watering, they drink moonlight. Get a bit moody in daylight, mind. You need to watch them around pets and small children.'

The moonflowers were facing the boys in a slightly menacing way. Baby Todd took hold of Elsie's hand.

'Known to nip,' added Evie. 'Not hard, but just keep an eye out.'

'Stand back, boys,' said Elsie. 'You heard the ladies. The flowers bite.'

'Nip,' corrected Evie. 'So, who are these dear little fellows?' She beamed down at the boys, tail swishing happily. The boys stared back, round-eyed, mouths open, struck dumb by tails, pails and flowers that might nip.

'My brothers,' said Elsie. 'Say hello, boys.' Arthy, Toby and Baby Todd squirmed shyly and said nothing. You could tell they were quite liking the attention, though.

'We weren't expecting to see you here, ladies,' said Joey.

'Oh, we like a market, don't we, Evie?' said Ada. 'Just the place for finding good homes for the moonflowers. We get overcrowded at the height of the growing season, the older ones have to move out. We never felt we'd be welcome in Smallbridge until today. But we heard on the grapevine that Magenta's opened a magic shop here so it seems the place isn't as stuffy as we thought.'

'Now we know why you steal buckets,' said Joey, sniffing the nearest moonflower, 'Wow, that smells ... odd.' The moonflower suddenly whipped round to face him, clearly offended. Hastily, Joey backed away.

'*Steal buckets*? We can't think what you mean, dear. *Do* consider giving a home to a moonflower. You can use them as a reading lamp. Just be careful not to sneak up on them.'

'They've got a dark side,' said her sister.

'Yes. Best placed back against a wall.'

They smiled beneath their frilly bonnets. Behind their skirts, their tails wagged to and fro. Nuisance bared his teeth. He didn't really didn't like the Howlers. They brought out the dog in him.

'Umm … we'll think about it,' fibbed Elsie. 'Anyway, we'd best get going. We're off to buy toffee apples.'

They walked on and soon came across another surprise. A tea stall. Rows of cups and saucers laid out, and presided over by a familiar large, yellow fortune-telling teapot. The sign out front said:

MADAME SHIRLEY, FORTUNE TELLER TO THE STARS. HAVE A CUPPA, KNOW YOUR FUTURE. 2 SHILLINGS. FREE BUN.

'Morning, dears,' said Shirley, beaming over the teapot. 'Surprised to see me again so soon?'

'A bit,' said Elsie. 'What's all this about?' She waved her hand around, taking in the sign, the stall, the tea cups, everything.

'What d'you think? A tea stall. Something this town badly needs. It's not only Madge that can come up with a clever little business venture. Now, unless you want tea and a reading, please move along so paying customers can get through.'

'I'd like a bun,' said Corbett hopefully.

'Buns only come with tea and a reading. Off you go.'

A bit further along, between a stall selling radishes and one selling cheese, was a small tent covered in faded mystic squiggles. A sign said:

WENDY SNIPE, WISE WOMAN OF CLACKHAM COMMON. TOP NOTCH WISDOM! REASONABLE RATES.

Elsie put her ear to the canvas. Inside the tent, Wendy was loudly telling Mrs Snoring that she'd be wise to go back to the Emporium because Albert Pickles had been quite right to throw unruly customers out of his shop, and besides, there was a sale on. Outside, Mrs Lardy, Miss Winnie Whippet and the two Old Trouts were waiting for a turn. All four smiled at Elsie. Mrs Lardy patted Nuisance and said she'd be calling in the Emporium later for soap powder and a pickle fork. The fight in the shop, it seemed, was forgotten.

'Wendy's doing good business,' said a voice from behind. Maureen was looming over them with a shopping basket full of vegetables. 'Shirley's popular too. Everyone likes a cuppa. This starting-up-a-business craze is really catching on. Almost tempted to give it a go myself.'

'What would you do?' asked Joey.

'General sort of haggery, I suppose. Cackling over candles sort of thing. What d'you reckon, Elsie?'

'Well,' said Elsie. 'Cackling over candles is a bit of a minority interest … but Smallbridge seems to be coming around to new ideas so who knows, maybe give it a go—'

She was cut off by the almighty crash of cymbals! Into the square marched a grim-faced collection of people. They consisted of: Angry Beard Man, Mr Sourman (on cymbals), the woman with a green hat, the one with a single eyebrow and the man with no chair at the council meeting. Between them, they carried a selection of unfriendly signs:

'Uh-oh!' croaked Corbett, from Joey's shoulder. 'This isn't good.'

Everyone in the market – stallholders and shoppers alike – stopped what they were doing and stared. Shirley put the lid on her teapot. Wendy's head poked out of her tent. Maureen put down her basket and folded her arms.

The group of protestors came to a halt and

formed a huddle. If it wasn't for the horrible signs and the grim faces, they could have been a choir about to break into song. Or perhaps not.

'Witches out!' bellowed angry beard man. 'Witches unwelcome!'

'Right!' piped up Mr Sourman. 'There's no place for witches here.'

'You'd be wise to take that back, dears,' said Wendy. 'Wouldn't they, Shirley?'

'They would,' said Shirley.

Suddenly, all the witches who had been wandering happily around the market were standing in a grim-faced line at the front. The jolly atmosphere was jolly no more.

'I don't like this,' Joey whispered in Elsie's ear. 'Can't you do something?'

'No,' said Elsie, looking on hopelessly. Tensions from the last few days were finally about to boil over and she hadn't a clue how to stop a big fight breaking out..

'But you've got the knack! Do your frogs or eggs. Freeze them or something.'

'Eggs and frogs won't help, Joey. I can't use baby spells on angry witches. They'd laugh in my face.'

'Don't try threatening us with your nasty, wicked magic!' shouted the woman with the green hat. 'We're citizens of Smallbridge and we can say what we like!'

'Well,' said Maureen crisply. 'We're witches, you see, and we can *do* what we like.'

'Oh, is that so?' bawled angry beard man. 'Think you can scare us? Coming here! Settling up shop! Corrupting our kids! Taking our money! Taking over *my town*!'

'Hear, hear,' chimed in his fellow protesters.

'Witches Go Home!'

'Ladies,' said Maureen, loking around at her fellow witches. Her right hand was moving to her voluminous left sleeve, where she kept her wand. 'I think we've heard enough, am I right?'

'Elsie,' said Joey. 'You have to do something. It's getting … too serious. Look, they're getting all their wands out!'

Elsie thought hard. She needed a distraction. Something that wouldn't hurt, or offend anyone. Something that would take away all the bad feeling and make everybody cheerful again. A rainbow? A sudden snow shower? Baskets of fluffy baby rabbits? All good, but wouldn't necessarily appeal to everybody...

Suddenly, she had it.

'Arthy,' she said. 'Can I have your pot of Tickle Dust, please? We're going to try it out!'

'Now?' squealed Arthy. He gave a little jump of happiness.

'Yes, now!'

Speechless with excitement, eyes shining, Arthy reached into his pocket, brought out the precious little gold pot and handed it to Elsie.

Elsie unscrewed it easily. Inside, it was packed to the brim with fine, sparkling golden dust, like powdered sunshine.

Right, she thought. *Let's hope it does what it says on the tin.*

'Okay, Arthy' she said. 'Now – count to three, take a deep breath, then blow.'

'One … two … six!' said Arthy. And blew.

And the tickle dust came out, in a glittering, swirling great puff of golden cloud!

The dust was smart. It knew what to do. It swirled in a golden stream over the heads of the

crowd, gathered itself up and rained
down gently on the heads and shoulders
of those who needed an extra dose – the
protesters.

Angry beard man looked startled – then his
brow smoothed, the lower half of his face creased
and slowly, he broke into a smile! Then, much
to his own surprise, he gave a rusty chuckle. It
was a sound he hadn't made in years.

Next to him, Mr Sourman let out a braying
little giggle, looked surprised, then did it again.
The woman in the green hat and her friend

with the single eyebrow both grinned from ear to ear. No-chair man made a funny hiccup sound. Then, simultaneously, they all dropped their signs, threw back their heads and burst into loud, hearty laughter!

In seconds, the entire market place was doubled up, witches and townsfolk alike. It was as though people hadn't laughed properly for years, and needed to let it all out. They giggled and gasped, held their stomachs and leaned on each others shoulders, shaking helplessly with mirth.

Tickle Dust. Hand crushed by jolly elves. It tickled you and made you happy. What incredible stuff.

Chapter Ten
WHAT NEXT?

Sylphine was as ready as she would ever be for her first-ever job interview. Elsie's mum had given her suit a sponge down – Arthy had spilled orange juice down it, Toby had pulled a button loose and baby Todd had wiped his nose on the hem. She had polished her horrible shoes and pinned back her hair.

'How do I look?' she asked Albert, who was busy sorting the till out.

'Very nice,' said Albert without really looking.

'You don't mind that I'm leaving you, do

you, Mr Pickles?'

'No,' said Albert. 'Not a bit, dear.'

'Because when I'm Magenta's assistant, you'll get Elsie back. Can I do anything for you? Before I go?'

'No, thank you, Sylphine. I'm fine.'

Sylphine went – then was back.

'It's not open.'

'Ah. Yes, come to think of it, Elsie did mention she thought Witch Sharp might open up later today.' Albert sounded a bit disapproving. The Emporium always opened on time. 'She'll lose a lot of trade that way. What are you doing with that key, dear?'

Sylphine had unhooked one of the keys that hung by the counter. It was the big red one for Sharp Spells that Magenta had given Elsie.

'I'm going to open up for Miss

Sharp,' she said. 'I'll pull up the shutters and get everything ready. I know how to do it now I've watched you.'

'I'm not sure—'

'It'll be a nice surprise, won't it? Miss Sharp will turn up and see me doing it all, serving customers and being helpful and that, and hire me on the spot. See you later, Mr Pickles.'

'I don't think … you in a magic shop—'

Too late. Sylphine was gone.

Sylphine stood in the doorway of Sharp Spells, gazing at the goods on display. A number of items woke up as the daylight filtered in, sensing a new day and more opportunities to do their thing, whatever that happened to be.

Fake snakes wiggled. Wands fizzed. The tailor's dummies stretched and rolled their shoulders.

Sylphine felt encouraged. So far, so good. She had managed to walk down the alley without tripping over or stepping in something nasty. She had gasped in admiration and excitement at the first sight of the wonderful new magic shop where she would shortly be working. Although, on closer inspection the exterior didn't look that great. Considering it was newly opened, it was looking a bit, well, tired. Not only had the four S's stopped twinkling, they had fallen off the sign. Yet another tile had slid off the roof and fallen to the cobbles when she unlocked the door.

But inside wasn't so bad. At least nothing had launched itself off a shelf and gone for her leg. There were stirrings and fizzles and the odd spark, but nothing too unsettling. Although you never knew what might happen around magic. She would be extra careful, just in case of mishap.

The shutters needed opening and the sign needed to be changed to **OPEN** – but first things first, Sylphine wanted to know what it felt like to stand behind the counter and be in charge. To be a real shop keeper.

She moved behind the counter and arranged herself in the sort of pose she had observed Albert adopt.

'Good morning, modom,' said Sylphine to the empty air. 'Is modom looking for anything special today?'

The empty air said nothing in return.

'Just arsk if you need any help, sir,' said Sylphine in Albert's very best, politest tones.

Stony silence.

Sylphine turned her attention to the till. It looked complicated – even more so than the one in the Emporium. The one that she'd got her hair caught up in. Perhaps she should leave it alone until she knew how to use it.

There was something under the till, though. A white envelope, addressed to Magenta. Sylphine frowned. Could this be an application for the shop assistant job? If so, she would dispose of it quickly.

Sylphine gave a shifty glance around, then tore open the envelope and quickly withdrew a single sheet of paper.

Dear Magenta,

I assume the Spellatron 3000 I ordered for you from the catalogue arrived safely. Knowing you, I wasn't expecting thanks. I thought it would suit you, as it operates with minimum input from the user and I know how lazy you are. Plus it doesn't smell or fizz or require the user to leap around a bonfire wearing riduculous red clothes. My hope was that as I can't persuade you to give up magic entirely, at least you might try something a little more civilised.

However, you've probably found out for yourself by now, the bad news is that the Spellatron 3000 is faulty. It seems the new magic doesn't work properly and the manufacturer is calling them back in. Loads of terrible reviews. They start off all right, then run out of steam. They look boring, you can't turn them off, things start to crumble and go wrong, all kinds of criticism. Unfortunately, when I ordered you one, I put your name down to pay for it. It wasn't cheap either. Well, maybe it will teach you that magic is a terrible thing and that you really should settle down and live a normal life.

Your loving sister

Gosh, thought Sylphine. *That's harsh. She and Granny would get on well.*

She stuffed the letter into her pocket. It was then that she suddenly became aware of a strange sound. A sort of weird, wheezy buzzing noise, coming from somewhere around her knees.

Sylphine bent down, reached into the darkness under the counter and carefully felt around. When she straightened, in her hands was a smooth, shiny, weird-looking thing the size and shape of a brick with a row of holes in the side. Three small, fierce red lights were pulsing on and off behind all the holes. Wonky-sounding buzzing came from somewhere deep inside.

This must be the The Spellatron 3000, thought Sylphine. Miss Sharp's sister was right, the device clearly wasn't at all well.

There came creaking and groaning sounds. Sylphine looked up. All around, horrible things were happening to the shop. The walls were bulging. The shelves were springing off the walls. The floor looked like it was moving up and down.

Sylphine was determined to treat the Spellatron 3000 very, very carefully. She would lower it - very slowly, little by little, onto the counter . . .

'WHAT EXACTLY DO YOU THINK YOU'RE DOING, SYLPHINE GREENMANTLE?!' barked a voice.

Sylphine gave a squeal, jumped and … dropped it! There was a sharp crack as the device bounced off the edge of the counter and fell to the floor with a nasty crunch.

There came an almighty explosion of

multi-coloured lights! Sparkles and twinkles and flashings like an accident in a firework factory but without the noise. This was a silent explosion.

Then, quietly and with no fuss, the shop disappeared. Simply vanished, along with everything in it.

Sylphine and Magenta found themselves standing knee-deep in nettles in Smallbridge's town dump. Alongside two old, abandoned armchairs and a broken spinning wheel. A short distance away, a small goat tethered to a post looked up and gave a mild bleat.

'Oops,' said Sylphine. At her feet lay the Spellatron 3000. It was silent. No lights, red or green, shone from the holes. She nudged it with

her shoe. No response.

'You silly girl!' hissed Magenta. 'You dropped it!'

'Yes,' said Sylphine. 'Yes. I did. Accidentally.'

'And now it's broken and my shop is gone! Think I've got time to waste rebuilding up a business from scratch?'

'Sorry. But it was playing up before I dropped it, Miss Sharp. I just sort of put it out of its misery. Um - I think you should read this.'

She reached into her pocket and handed over the crumpled letter.

'Well,' said Magenta, after reading it. 'That's nice. Typical of my sister, sending me something faulty. and expecting me to pay for it. What are you doing in my shop anyway?'

'I was going to apply for the shop-assistant job. But I don't suppose you'll need one now there's no shop to assist in. Granny's going to be furious.' Sylphine gave a sniffle. 'I'm sorry, Miss Sharp.'

'Oh, stop looking so droopy!' Magenta gave a sigh and plumped down in an old armchair, which puffed out ancient dust. 'You've probably done both of us a favour. You'd make a terrible assistant and I've had more than enough of shop keeping. No customers on the first day, three annoying ones on the second, and mobbed on the third. It's either boring, irritating or exhausting. I don't know how Elsie and her dad stand it. No, best that I pack it in and go back home to Crookfinger. What's that down in the grass by your horrible shoe?'

It was a single small, gold pot with a red jewel on the lid.

'It seems the shop left one thing behind,' said

Magenta, picking up the pot. 'Tickle Dust. I was wondering what it was like, actually. It was very popular. Shall we give it a try?'

Epilogue
BACK TO NORMAL

'I've never seen her actually laugh before,' said Sylphine. 'That Tickle Dust is really something. I wish I'd bought loads.'

'Did you use all of it?' asked Elsie.

'No. But I dropped the pot on the way home. Have you ever seen laughing rabbits? I have.'

'You should have been at the market,' said Joey. 'Everyone was splitting their sides. I actually hurt I laughed so much. Bill got all his wires in a twist. It was just one gigantic laugh-in.'

'That's the thing about laughter,' said Elsie. 'Everyone likes it, so it spreads.'

It was one week after the market incident and the disappearance of the Sharp Spells shop. The three friends, plus Nuisance and Bill, had arranged to meet on the common and were standing looking at the space where the tower now wasn't.

'I felt really bad about her shop,' said Sylphine, who was back to her old self – wafty green gown and tangled hair with flowers in. Her granny had finally given up on her. 'She didn't seem too cross, though. Even after the Tickle Dust stopped working. '

'Don't feel bad,' said Elsie. 'Magenta's not suited to shop keeping. Or to town life. She'll be much happier back in the forest. So will Corbett. And the tower will stop being on

strike and start giving them cake again.'

'What about the town?' asked Joey. 'It's had a bit of a shake-up. Will Smallbridge go back to normal?'

'It's back to normal already,' said Elsie. 'The mayor's come out of hiding and pretends not to know what people are talking about when they ask him about the toad. All the Emporium's regulars are back and Mr Sourman wrote a note apologising for his behaviour. It seems the Tickle Dust did him a lot of good. He lives on his own and he's a bit lonely. He needed a good laugh. I expect Dad'll forgive him, if he pays for the stuff he stole. Talking of Dad, I must get back. It's nearly opening time.'

'Are you taking a shortcut?' asked Joey.

'No. I'm going to be cutting back on those for now. The problems with the Spellatron 3000 shows that shortcuts really aren't always the best idea. Much better to do things properly and take your time.'

'Fair enough. Bill and I had better make a start on the round.'

'And I must get back home to fill the bird feeders and wash my hair,' said Sylphine.

Nuisance gave a little yap. He was planning to go to the shop with Elsie. Maybe get an extra sausage.

So Joey and Sylphine went on their way and Elsie and Nuisance went home to Smallbridge – which, despite what Elsie said, wasn't quite the same.

There were now three sturdy benches in the square, a small, sparkling lemonade fountain, and a slightly scorched sheep statue that was crowned with a small pointy hat.

Also, Smallbridge was no longer so witchist. Even though *Sharp Spells The Shop* was closed, witches were still visiting the village, having become fans of the Emporium and the other shops on offer. Now the people of Smallbridge nodded at them in a friendly way, and some even waved and stopped for a quick chat.

Sometimes, Shirley appeared at the market and sold readings, buns and cups of tea. Several easily-persuaded people had given a home to a moonflower, and now read, knitted, or kissed their toddler's nipped fingers better every night by the moonlight of the flowers.

The children eked out their precious little pots of Tickle Dust, which meant there were often outbursts of unexpected laughter. In fact, the laughter bursts continued to happen, even after the Tickle Dust ran out.

And that, as Elsie said to Nuisance, could only be a good thing.

Acknowledgements

The terrific team at Simon and Schuster, especially my lovely editor, Jane. Ashley, my talented illustrator who has brought Elsie's world to life. My good friend and fantastic literary agent, Caroline Sheldon. My always supportive husband Mo and daughter Ella. All my loyal readers, young and not so young. All the bookshops and libraries who buy this book. The cats who let me cuddle them whenever I get stuck.

Even a witch needs a wish every once in a while!

KAYE UMANSKY

Wish for a Witch

illustrated by ASHLEY KING

Book two out now!